"A bold and daring new voice in the thriller genre, Doris Pariso's debut is one readers will not want to end. *Run! Katie!* is filled with twists and turns, leaving you feeling as if you are living the protagonist's every thought and action and anticipating what's coming while on the edge of your seat. This book is a thrilling must-read mystery woven with the beautiful story of everlasting love between mother and daughter."

> —**Dianne C. Braley**, Author of *The Silence in the Sound*, Winner of the 2022 NYC Big Book Award and Pencraft Award for Women's Fiction

"*Run! Katie!* is a carefully crafted tale that aligns its thrills with the roots of deep family connection. Author Pariso keeps the reader intrigued by unraveling the accounts of a chilling mystery that begs to be solved. Highly recommend."

> —**Mario Rutledge,** Author of *No Gun Intended*

"A fine first novel with a fascinating theme."

> —**Nicholas Harvey,** *USA Today* Best-Selling Author

"I loved this book! The characters were so real and believable! I enjoyed the twists and turns in the plot, too."

> —**Kim Arnold,** Author and Retired Librarian/Teacher

"As a former suspect in a small-town scandal comes back to town, we jump in to an intense, all-too-relatable mystery about a young woman who doesn't realize she is being watched. At a point in her life when she's finally adjusting to her mother's disappearance, Katie now unknowingly finds herself caught back in the web of danger. Can she be saved? Or will Katie suffer the same fate as her mother? With the help of a medium, we see that a mother's love knows no bounds, as she conspires with some unlikely help to save Katie and reveal the truth. This story takes you on an adrenaline[-fueled] roller coaster as you feel just as vulnerable as Katie. Pariso may be new to the novel scene, but with plot twists like this, watch out; [this] won't be her last!"

—Nichole Inthanongsak, Home School Educator

"I loved this book. I did not want to put it down. It was a real page-turner. I would definitely recommend this book to my friends and family."

—Linda Maloney, Registered Nurse

"Doris Pariso's first foray has nailed the thriller [genre], and fans of this genre will be immediately drawn into this book by the intrigue and mystery surrounding the characters. The plot twists and turns that hinge on the visions of a psychic provide suspense while giving the reader an urgency to learn the outcome. A definite must-read!"

—Karen Whitman, Speech Therapist

"I give five stars to this well-told story from this new author! Settle in and enjoy it from the captivating beginning to its happy ending. . . . [W]ith richly developed characters . . . this book leaves me wanting more. I have no doubt that you will be fascinated by Doris Pariso's book. This author is definitely one to watch!"

—Louise Levasseur, Retired Director of
Supply Chain Lenze America

Run! Katie!

by Doris Pariso

© Copyright 2023 Doris Pariso

ISBN 978-1-64663-997-7

Published by

köehlerbooks™

3705 Shore Drive
Virginia Beach, VA 23455

800-435-4811

Run! Katie!

———— • ————

DORIS PARISO

Doug,
Happy reading!
Doris Pariso

VIRGINIA BEACH
CAPE CHARLES

Dedicated with love to my husband Bart

&

in memory of Susan
(1963-2022),

a friend for the ages.

PROLOGUE

———•◆•———

Friday, November 11, 2005

BRRRRNNNGGGG! BRRRRRNNNGGG! The ring of the alarm clock shook Katie from a deep sleep. With her eyes barely opened, she struggled to her feet and shuffled along the hardwood floor toward the obnoxiously loud ringing. Since it was Friday, she was not dreading getting out of bed. Not only was Friday the last day of school before the weekend, but on Fridays, her dad returned home from the city to spend the weekend with her and her mom, not to mention her mom made Katie's favorite breakfast of pancakes and bacon.

Katie quickly made her way to the bathroom, where she washed up, brushed her teeth, and fixed her hair. She returned to her bedroom and got dressed. After haphazardly making her bed, she headed downstairs. Halfway down the steps, she was surprised by the silence and the absence of the smell of food coming from the kitchen.

"Mom!" she shouted.

Silence.

"Mom!" she shouted a bit louder.

Silence.

She entered the empty kitchen, still calling out for her mom. She turned back and bounded up the stairs to her mom's bedroom.

"Mom! Mom!"

She opened the door. All she found was a neatly made bed in the empty room.

"Mom! Mom!"

Silence.

She continued making her way through the house, checking the bathroom and art room. Both rooms were empty.

"Mom!"

Silence.

With panic beginning to rise, she made her way back downstairs.

"Mom! Mom! Where are you?"

Silence.

Entering the kitchen for a second time, she grabbed an apple from the fruit bowl on the island, holding it as she would a baseball ready to be thrown. She proceeded to check out the rest of the house.

Every room was empty, and all shouts were met with nothing but silence. She unlocked and opened the door to the garage. Her mom's car was there. Fighting back the tears that were welling up in her eyes, she ran to the phone and called her dad.

"Good morning," her dad's voice boomed.

"Dad! Dad! Where's Mom?"

"What do you mean, where's Mom?" he replied. "She is home with you."

"She's not here!" Katie answered in a shaky voice. "Her car is here, but she is not!"

"She must be there, honey."

Katie could no longer hold back the tears as she spoke into the phone.

"She's gone, Dad! She's gone!"

Friday

———•———

OCTOBER 20, 2017

One

*K*eep running! *Keep running!* The words echo in her head. Legs heavy, no voice. Can't run. Can't scream. He's coming. She can feel his breath. He's right behind her. *Run! Scream!* Nothing. Legs of lead. Voice silent.

She awakens abruptly, covered in sweat, both fists clinched so tightly that her nails are making an imprint on her palms. She sits straight-up, catches her breath, and slowly returns to reality.

"It was a dream. Just a dream." She allows her eyes to adjust to the dark room before reaching for her phone. The clock on her phone reaffirms what she already knows. It is 3:24. Of course, it is . . . it's always 3:24.

♦ ♦ ♦

BRRRRNNNGGGG! BRRRRRNNNGGG! The familiar but annoying sound was blaring from the out-of-date alarm clock on the dresser in Katie's small bedroom. Katie knew all too well that the antiquated clock, which had once belonged to her mother and her grandmother before that, would continue to scream at her until she put an end to it. The treasured alarm clock was given to her on her tenth birthday, twelve years ago to the day, but the memory was as fresh in Katie's mind as if it happened only yesterday.

"This is a rite of passage," her mom had told her. "You are a big girl now and no longer need me to wake you up," she continued with a smile. "This will get the job done just fine. It is the first clock your great-grandfather ever made, and though it won't wake you up to music like those fancy-schmancy clock radios, it will most definitely wake you up! I can attest to that! It might wake up the entire neighborhood!"

Her mom accompanied the gift with a bit of motherly advice, which, all these years later, Katie still followed. She bent to Katie's level with a look that said she was about to share the secret of the meaning of life with her. Slowly, she said, "Put the alarm clock on the far side of the room so that you have to get out of bed to shut it off."

With the alarm persistently ringing, Katie begrudgingly threw the covers off her petite body and stumbled, her eyes barely opened, toward the last gift her mother had given her. Because of the size of the room, the dresser was only a few stumbles away. If she was taller than five foot one, she might not have to get out of bed to put a stop to the incessant ringing. As badly as she wanted to hit the source of the noise hard enough to ensure that it would never ring again, she did as she does every morning. She gently picked up the clock, pushed the button to quiet it, looked at the moving hands, and said in a soft voice, "Good morning, Mom, wherever you are." She smiled with a tear in her eye as she remembered that morning, twelve years ago, while holding the now quiet clock tightly to her chest. It seemed to tick in rhythm with her heart, as if it was beating for her.

"Twelve years?" she whispered to herself. "Has it really been twelve years?" Her question hung in the otherwise silent room. In some ways, the years had passed quickly, a rapid string of events, almost a blur, but other memories and events seemed to play in her head over and over in slow motion, like a paused image on a TV screen—frozen in time, perfectly still, unchanging, haunting her.

It wasn't just the images in her mind that haunted her. There were the nightmares—the vivid, all-too-real nightmares—which had recently become a nightly occurrence. In the first few years following her mom's disappearance, nightmares cluttered her sleep, but in recent years, she had enjoyed a dream-free sleep— until two weeks ago, when that came to an abrupt halt.

Accompanying the nightmares was an unsettling feeling in the pit of her stomach. It was as if her gut was yelling at her, trying desperately to warn her of an impending danger. Not just warn her but protect her. The feeling combined with the nightmares left her a bit unnerved and tired, but this morning, she was determined to get an early start. With the alarm silenced, Katie set about getting prepared for her morning run. A glance toward the open door of the other bedroom found the bed undisturbed. "Hmmm, someone didn't make it home last night," Katie said, chuckling to herself.

Ally, her outgoing and fun-loving roommate, told her she probably wouldn't be back until morning. Part of Ally's job at the college was planning and preparing student events. For months, she was actively involved in the planning and setup for this weekend's festival. The thought of the upcoming Fall Fest added a zip to Katie's step, not because she was excited for this weekend like everyone else seemed to be, but because she was motivated to get her morning run in while the campus and surrounding town were quiet and virtually empty. She was well aware that, after this morning, it would be days before any semblance of normalcy occurred again. She did not know how right she was.

Dressed in shorts and a brightly colored T-shirt, she pulled her long brown hair into a scrunchy, tied the laces on her worn running shoes, and headed out the door. The crisp autumn air completed the job her alarm clock had started. Within a few minutes, she was fully awake and jogging along the familiar route.

Being that today was her twenty-second birthday and almost twelve years since she had last seen her mom, it did not surprise her that she was feeling hyperemotional, which resulted in both her thoughts and her feet racing faster than usual. With each stride, the memories came rushing in, the same set of memories that played in her mind whenever she allowed herself to remember. Besides fondly recalling her mom giving her the alarm clock, she did not allow herself to remember much else that occurred before that fateful, life-altering morning.

Time had taught Katie that when someone you love simply vanishes from your life in a sudden, unexplained manner, it invalidated all the years before it. They take with them not only the future but the past. It makes every moment shared with them seem void, fraudulent, and sad—unbearably sad, so sad that it is easier not to remember, easier to bury the memories deep down, where they can be locked away, as if in an impenetrable box, except for the exceedingly rare, unexpected, vulnerable moment, in which a faded memory would rise to the surface. For a moment, it would put a smile on her face and warm her heart, but those feelings were quickly followed by an intense emptiness and hurt, which would shake her body to the core.

Fueled by brilliant sunshine, pleasantly warm temperatures, and an unexplained abundance of energy, Katie extended her run to include the path that ran alongside the lake. With each stride she took, the surrounding beauty added to her energetic mood. It was during the months immediately following her mom's mysterious disappearance that she took to running. What began as an outburst from an angry and confused ten-year-old—a desperate attempt to run away from everything, including her own pain and confusion—was cultivated into the best therapy Katie had ever received.

She discovered that running could either run the thoughts out of her head or, if she was really lucky, allow her to resolve her current dilemma. Before she knew it, running became a part of her daily routine. The alarm ringing was her signal to get up and run. Her Aunt Patty called her "the mailman of running. Not rain, sleet, or snow could deter her."

A smile appeared on her reddened face as she remembered the times when Aunt Patty or her dad would accompany her on one of her morning runs. Try as they might, they could not keep up. Katie would show kindness for a while but did not take pity for too long. About fifteen minutes into the jog, with a grin and a nod of her head, her short but powerful legs would begin churning, and in a matter of moments, she was out of their sight.

It was during these runs that she was able to come to terms with the anger and pain of so much loss and so many unanswered questions. She credited her running habit for bringing her to the place she now found herself—a place of contentment and even happiness that she had enjoyed in recent years. That is what made the nightmares and the unsettling feeling in the pit of her stomach even more troublesome and confusing. As she continued the brisk pace along the shore of the lake, something told her she couldn't run from these feelings.

Two

It was with a mix of excitement and trepidation that Katie set about getting ready for the birthday luncheon with her dad, Aunt Patty, and, of course, Ally. That is if Ally made it in time. She loved her dad and her aunt very much. She appreciated all they had done for her and was looking forward to seeing them. However, she dreaded the underlying notes of sadness they shared—a sadness created by so many unanswered questions, combined with the ever-present guilt Katie felt for leaving Harperstown and them behind. She was aware of the sacrifices both Patty and her dad had made to assure that she could grow up in Harperstown. After Sharon disappeared, Patty was not only willing but eager to help John raise her sister's only child, assuring that her life was not turned completely upside down by leaving the home and life she'd always known.

As much as Katie appreciated their efforts to keep her in her home, by the time she had reached the age of sixteen, she wanted nothing more than to get out of Harperstown, to live in a place where she was not the center of the town mystery, always gawked at or pitied, always in proximity to the whispers behind her back. She just wanted to be anywhere else, anywhere where she could just be plain Katie.

As badly as she longed to leave Harperstown and her past behind, deep inside, she knew she could not go too far, could not cut the ties completely. She found the answer a little over an hour away at a quiet little campus that offered everything she needed and wanted.

It was during her four years at Barton College that she found some long sought-after peace and contentment, along with her first ever best friend. Her friendship with Ally is a true testament to the saying "Opposites attract." Unlike Katie, Ally lived a charmed life, which made her outgoing, trusting, friendly, and perpetually happy.

The unlikely pair met in a psychology class during their second semester. They were in the same group for a project and had an instant connection. When the time came to select next year's room assignment, Katie surprised herself by trading in her treasured single dorm room to room with Ally. They have been roomies ever since, even upon transitioning from dorms to an apartment. Ally took a job at the college after graduation, while Katie opted for a five-year program that would result in both a bachelor's and master's degree.

The sound of her phone vibrating on the table grabbed Katie's attention. She answered the phone, positioned the Bluetooth in her ear, and greeted her father. "Hey, Dad, what's up?" She talked while putting the finishing touches on her makeup. Her dad spoke with a hint of frustration. "Well, hello there, birthday girl! It appears this beautiful weather has brought everyone out. We might be a bit late, but we will be there." Katie knew it was the traffic, not her, that he was annoyed with.

"Don't worry. I can get there and hold our table. You just drive safe and enjoy the scenery," Katie instructed her dad with a smile. Before she ended the call, she heard Patty enthusiastically yell out, "Happy birthday!"

◆ ◆ ◆

From his seat at the end of the bar, Peter had a good view of the door. He could tell by the looks from some of the other patrons that they recognized him, thought they knew him, or thought he looked familiar but couldn't place who he was or how they knew him. He was especially grateful for anonymity today; he needed to be entirely focused on what he was here to do and did not want any frivolous distractions.

Peter spotted her as soon as she entered the restaurant and watched her as she followed the hostess to her seat. He knew it was her right away. Her image had been flashing in his mind since he took his seat on the wooden stool. He swallowed hard, attempting to clear his throat of the apple-sized lump that had formed there. She was only seated at her table for a couple of minutes when he approached her.

"Excuse me. I am sorry to interrupt," he said while reaching out his hand. "My name is Peter Dorjen, and I believe I have a message for you."

Katie's heart skipped a beat. From her experiences, messages from strange people rarely brought welcome news. She held her breath, thinking of her dad and Patty driving in. *Please let them be okay. Please!*

"A message for me?"

"Yes, if you are Kate?"

"I am Katie," she almost whispered in return.

"I know this will sound crazy, but I have been sent here to give you a message."

"Who? Who sent you?" *Don't be bad news. Don't be bad news.*

"Sharon, your mom, Sharon, sent me."

Katie gave a weak nod and waited for him to continue.

"She wanted me to give you a message. Your mom has passed, correct?"

"I thought so, but if she has given you a message to give to me, then I must be wrong."

"Quite the contrary. The fact that she has sent me a message to give to you means she has most definitely passed."

Three

Peter knew his words had startled Katie more than a little. He spoke softly, trying not to startle her any more than he already had. "I am sorry to just show up like this. As I said before, my name is Peter Dorjen. I am a psychic. Normally people schedule readings with me or book me to do events or parties." He handed her his card. "Your mom seems to have sought me out and has sent me to you. I believe she wants me to tell you some things," he said while pulling a chair out. "May I?"

"Yes," Katie said, nodding weakly.

Peter paused for a moment before continuing, "First, she wants me to wish you a happy birthday, or at least I believe that is what she wants, judging by the streamers, balloons, and a birthday cake that has your name on it. She also wants me to thank you for your loving greeting every morning as you turn your alarm off."

"D-d-d-id Ally send you here?" Katie struggled to get the words out.

"I don't know who Ally is. As I told you, Sharon sent me, and I might add, she was relentless in her pestering and insistence that I come see you today. She made it quite clear that she would not take no for an answer. At least if I ever wanted a good night's sleep."

Just as he finished the sentence, Ally joined them at the table. Patty and Katie's dad, John, were right behind her, making their way past the crowd around the bar. As soon as they reached the table, which offered a beautiful view of the lake, Patty pointed toward Peter and asked, "What is he doing here?"

Katie replied, "Mom sent him."

This elicited a baffled, "What did you say?" from her aunt, who had recognized the well-known and respected psychic right away. Over the years, Patty had been told by many people that he was a gifted psychic, so in the months following her sister's sudden disappearance, at the encouragement of friends and in a desperate attempt to get some answers, she attended a couple of his group readings. To her disappointment, he never did a reading on her. He looked her way once, and her heart skipped a beat as she awaited his words, but with a strange look on his face, he quickly looked the other way.

It was Patty's idea to have someone write down everything he said. At both events she attended, before Peter came out, a lady, who was there to introduce him, presented the crowd with a set of instructions. "Make sure you have something to write with and, of course, something to write on. Also, have a partner at the ready, so if needed, they can write for you, or you can write for them. Remember to take down everything Mr. Dorjen says during his reading. Try to record everything. Some things he says may not make sense or they may seem unimportant now but may make a good deal of sense or seem relevant later. The words come fast and furious, and it is amazing what you may not recall down the road."

Remembering these instructions from years ago, Patty suggested that somebody take notes. Ally eagerly obliged to Patty's request. She stood up, walked across the crowded restaurant, and quickly returned with a pen and pad in hand. "I will be happy to play secretary. I knew all that note-taking in school would come in handy someday," she said with a laugh.

Patty's look of excitement and anticipation was equaled only by John's look of skepticism. He hoped that this, whatever this was, did not ruin Katie's birthday. She had already experienced a lifetime's worth of pain, and, with Peter in front of her, she looked as white as one of the ghosts this fellow was supposedly talking with. As if he read John's mind, Peter turned his attention toward him. "I am seeing the opening of the cartoon *The Jetsons*. George and Jane are communicating with each other using a futuristic computer. She is at home, and he is at work. I feel as if I should call you . . . George."

John's head felt light and as if it were spinning; all the activity in the noisy room seemed to come to an abrupt halt. *What did he just say? How? Why would he say that? Nobody could have told this Peter guy to say that . . . nobody except Sharon or Patty.*

Shortly after Katie was born, John was offered a fantastic career opportunity in a city two and a half hours away from their home, but this posed a bit of a dilemma. Sharon and John both wanted to live in Harperstown. To raise their family in the quaint little lake town where Sharon spent her childhood years, John would have to spend weekdays in the city and come home on weekends. Due to the high salary that came with the job, combined with the sizeable inheritance he, being an only child, received when his parents lost their lives in a tragic accident, money was not an issue. Staying close as a couple and family was their only concern, but that was quickly and easily resolved.

Thanks to John's computer savvy and the generosity of the company he was working with, they were one of the first couples to use computers to bridge the distance through email and chat rooms.

After putting Katie down for the night, Sharon would brew herself a cup of tea and sit down at the computer. Smiling with anticipation, she would communicate with John. By today's standards, what Sharon and John endured to get one message was arduous and slow, but it was an amazing lifeline for them.

Sharon used to joke that she could make her marriage work because she was living like Jane Jetson. When communicating through the computer, she referred to him as George.

"George! Did he say George?" Patty asked no one in particular.

"Yes, he did," John replied, staring at Peter, suddenly hungry for more. "Yes, he did!"

"She wants you to know that she loved you then, loves you now, and will love you until the sun no longer shines." Hearing Peter say the exact words he had spoken to her on the day he proposed sent a chill up his spine. Aware of the emotions John was feeling, Peter gave him a few seconds to digest his words before he spoke again. "She is telling me you need to go through her memories." Peter paused for a second before continuing, "You need to share them with Katie."

Nothing of what he was saying made any sense to Peter, but it was obvious to him that the words had really rattled John or George, or whatever his name was. Patty, who also looked a bit shaken, was hanging onto Peter's every word. With growing anticipation of what he, or more accurately, Sharon, would say next, she found the simple task of breathing required thought and conscious effort. It was while she was trying to bring air into her lungs that Peter turned his attention toward her.

"She wants me to thank you for helping to take such wonderful care of sweet, sweet Kate. She is smiling and wants me to tell you she couldn't have done a better job herself." Peter was amazed at the clarity of the messages he was receiving from Sharon. "Now, she says, it's time for you to get a life, sista." The phrase sounded funny coming from Peter, but in Patty's head, she heard her sister saying it, with her unique emphasis on the word *sista*. "She is grinning from ear to ear," he added unnecessarily. Patty, along with John, knew full well that statement was founded in humor and love. More importantly, they also felt strangely certain that it had come from Sharon. They just did not know how or why. *Why now? Why today? Why him?*

Four

With the table suddenly quiet, the server, who had been waved away a few times by Ally, cautiously approached one more time. He promptly took their drink orders, along with an order of appetizers for the table, which included a double order of Katie's favorite buffalo chicken rolls. They encouraged Peter to stay for lunch. He resisted at first, insisting that they should be left alone to celebrate Katie's birthday, but in the end, he relented and ordered a glass of red wine fermented and made at one of his favorite wineries, which was located a few miles up the road. He made a mental note to stop there on his way home to buy a bottle or two. If this past couple of weeks was any indication of things to come, he would be glad he did.

Lunch was delicious, and animated conversation filled the room. It was the type of conversation that happens when a group of people who have not seen each other in a while gets together. Peter informed them that Sharon was no longer communicating with him, and he no longer felt her presence. It took a bit for them to put aside what had just occurred, but in a short period of time, the small group was enjoying the food while exchanging stories and smiles.

"Let's see . . . why are we here? Oh, yeah, it is my baby girl's birthday, and with birthdays comes presents." John pulled a neatly wrapped package out of his coat pocket and handed it to Katie. "Happy birthday, sweetheart!" Katie excitedly tore the wrapping paper off and opened the box. She gasped as she looked down at a beautifully colored opal.

"You do know that is your birthstone, don't you?"

"I do. I am just surprised you do! Thank you, Dad. It is beautiful!"

"It is gorgeous!" Ally said while helping her friend clasp the necklace.

"My turn! My turn!" Patty chimed in and handed Katie a box that was a little bigger than the one her father gave her.

Katie was obviously pleased with Patty's gift, a runner's armband with a device that would not only play music but keep track of her distance, time, and route. Katie was never too concerned with how far or fast she ran, but Patty was always interested. It amazed her aunt that she never joined a track team. God knows the girl could run! Years ago, Patty gave up pestering her to join a team, but she still knew how important running was to Katie and continued to encourage and support her.

"That's not all. Look in the box." Katie reached in and pulled out a gift certificate to her favorite sporting goods store.

"Thank you so much, Patty. I have pretty much run the soles off the bottom of my old shoes!"

"That leaves me," Ally said cheerfully. "And I may need to borrow that armband," she said as she handed Ally a sheet of paper. Katie's face broke into a smile as she read the registration form for the upcoming marathon to benefit a local food pantry.

"You're going to run a marathon?"

"Not exactly. . . . *We* are going to run a marathon. I registered both of us."

"Oh, I would run three marathons just to see you run one!" Katie sounded amused. "Thanks, everyone. It has been a wonderful birthday!" She stood up and hugged Ally and Patty. While bending down to give her dad a thank-you hug, she looked up and gave Peter an appreciative smile, which told him that the messages he delivered today were the best gift of all.

Peter had thoroughly enjoyed the afternoon he spent with Sharon's family. He managed to put aside the uneasy feeling he had seeking this family out to speak the words of Mrs. Parish. He was also able to ignore the confusion he had when looking at Patty long enough to enjoy the meal and birthday celebration, confident that Patty was oblivious to his reaction when he first looked her way because she was so engrossed in the messages from her sister. He was glad she had the younger girl write everything down because he was certain she would not remember much of anything he said. As pleased as he was with the events of the afternoon, he could not forget what he saw—or what he didn't see—when looking at Patty. That had only happened to him one other time, and it rattled him then every bit as much as it did today.

Five

——— •◆• ———

Peter more than fulfilled the promise he made to himself and paid a visit to not just one but two of his favorite wineries on the way home. The sun was dropping lower on the horizon as he enjoyed a glass of his favorite dry red wines while sitting in the oversized Adirondack chair on the large deck of his home, which provided the perfect view of the lake below. He looked at a good deal of houses on the bigger lake, but after much consideration, he opted for the seclusion of the small lake over the crowds of one of the larger lakes. He much preferred canoes and kayaks to motorboats, which made the smaller lake a perfect fit for him. Plus, he loved the view, the breathtaking, gorgeous view.

He had looked at what seemed like hundreds of homes before he found the perfect one. As soon as he pulled up to his future home with his real estate agent, he looked at her and said with certainty, "This is the one."

"Don't you think we should check it out first?"

"Did you forget? I am a psychic," he teased.

They took the obligatory but unnecessary tour, and it only confirmed what Peter already knew; he had found his home. The events that followed continued to confirm Peter's hunch that this place was destined to be his home. The process could not have gone any smoother. Four weeks from the first time he stepped foot into the house, Peter was enjoying his first night in his new home. He actually liked that it was a half an hour from his office. It allowed for a separation from his "work" life and his "life" life, as he referred to them. Although, as this weekend reminded him, he could never fully separate the two.

Working on his second glass of wine, he reflected on the

events of the past two weeks and the lunch with Katie. Just when he thought he had reached an area of complete ease and comfort with his gift, this occurred. The fact that Sharon was the first spirit that ever sought him out—the first voice he ever heard—both startled and baffled him. Although he only heard her voice sporadically, he often knew that she was talking, but he couldn't make out what she was saying. When he could decipher her words, they were either simple phrases or a panicked command combined with images and feelings. At lunch, everything seemed so clear to him, clearer than ever before. This entire experience was unknown territory for him and had him wondering if he was going crazy.

From the time he could remember, he saw things others did not see. More accurately, he saw colors and sometimes images around people's bodies and heads. When he was young, he just assumed that was how people appeared to everyone, not just him. One day, he asked his mom why she was so red. He was five years old. They were in the kitchen making a batch of chocolate chip cookies. He was licking a sizeable chunk of cookie dough off the end of his finger when he asked her "the question," as she later referred to it.

"Why are you so red today?" he asked innocently.

She smiled. "Red. Don't you mean blue? But I'm not sure why you would ask that because I am not sad at all." She giggled and smudged some cookie dough on his nose.

"No, I mean red. You are very red today. What color am I?" he asked eagerly.

More than a little puzzled, his mom responded, "Well . . . your sweatpants are black, and your shirt is gray and black, so I guess you're gray and black today."

"No, I mean, what colors are around me?"

"Colors around you? I am not sure what you mean, honey."

He swept his tiny little hand through the air around his

mother's head. "These colors. The ones around our heads and bodies. What colors are around me today? I can't see the colors around me."

Baffled but slightly intrigued, she lifted him up onto the table and quizzed him about the colors and other things he saw. She reacted the way many mothers might by scheduling an eye appointment for him.

After being given the all clear by three eye doctors, she did not give his statement about seeing colors much more thought, except when her curiosity would get the best of her, and she would inquire what colors he saw around certain people. Within a short period of time, she recognized that her son had an extraordinary gift, a gift that she did not understand and found more than a bit unnerving. However, upon his persistent requests, she helped him research auras and what the various colors meant.

This research not only comforted but fascinated her. She began calling him out when she had company over, asking him to tell the ladies what colors and images he saw around them and what they meant. The more he did these impromptu readings, the better he got at them. He also developed what he referred to as an *instinct* that enabled him to put the images and colors together to form a picture of the person's past, present, and future. This was how his very unusual career began.

Word quickly spread of Peter and his gift, and people offered to pay him to come to their house to read people at gatherings. There were also those who would pay him for a private reading. By the time he was twenty-two, he was making over six figures and knew he had found his calling.

He had not heard Sharon's voice or even felt her presence since lunch, which, strange as it seemed, left him feeling kind of lonely. "Well, at least I should get some sleep tonight." He spoke to himself, a habit he had developed living alone all these years.

Sometimes he would catch himself doing it in public places, like the grocery store, but he quickly discovered that one perk of doing what he did for a living was that people did not question when he behaved strangely. In fact, they seemed to expect it.

Although it felt great to get a good night's sleep, Peter woke with an intense feeling of loneliness. He grinned at the absurdity of the fact that he actually missed the bombardment of images and Sharon's voice in his head. For him, it was the closest thing to pillow talk he had experienced in what seemed like forever. He had learned to accept that life without a partner was a downfall of his gift, a gift that had brought him so much joy and a life full of adventure and hope. He knew he had no choice but to embrace the gift that God had given him, even if it meant that he would never know the embrace of a wife.

How could he ever have an equal relationship with someone when he could read their moods and see things about them and their life that even they did not know? He discovered many years ago that he couldn't and had long since accepted it, or so he believed, but something in Sharon's presence, or lack thereof, caused an emptiness within him to rise to the surface. He would have reveled in the quiet solitude if he only knew how short-lived it would be.

Six

————•◆•————

During his first trip to Harperstown two weeks ago, Ethan was fighting an unrelenting urge to turn around. Until that trip, he had avoided this town he left almost twelve years ago. Although he hadn't been thrilled about returning to Harperstown, much less that house, time had erased some of his pain and anger, and now that he was buying his own house, he wanted some of his mom's things and items from his childhood in it. On his first visit to Harperstown a couple weeks earlier, he was certain that he didn't want to stay at Edward's house, so he booked a room at a nearby hotel.

Spending money on a hotel room was a bit out of the norm for him, but at the time, he just couldn't bear the thought of staying in that house with that man. Not that he was bad or abusive or anything. He just didn't like him. Never had and was pretty sure he never would. How could he ever like the town or the man? The town and the man had changed everything, torn his world apart, and ripped his mom from his life. The man and the town had escorted in what he referred to as "the dark years" of his life. To say coming back to this place was something he had dreaded would be an understatement, but it was something he knew he had to do. It was something years of counseling had prepared him for, or so he hoped.

He was certain that he may very well have turned around during that first trip two weeks earlier, but that option was taken away from him when his beater of a car stopped running. It did not just quietly stop but made a loud noise and abruptly stopped. With Ethan's knowledge of automobiles being minimal, to say the least, he reluctantly placed a call to Edward, who was surprisingly helpful. He asked him where he was and said he would head right over.

Ethan recognized the car as soon as Edward pulled up behind him. The sight of it took his breath away. Edward was driving Ethan's mom's old car, a black 535i BMW. He had just assumed that Edward sold the car years ago. During a rare phone call, Edward had offered the car to Ethan as a graduation present, but Ethan declined the offer. He wanted nothing from that man, especially the car Edward gave his mom as a wedding gift.

Seeing it pull up behind him brought back memories, many wonderful memories, like his mom picking him up after school, the two of them going for ice cream or to the bookstore. He wondered why he had not taken the car years ago, which made saying yes to Edward's suggestion that he use his mom's old car until his car was fixed easy to agree with. The car situation worked out very well, enabling Ethan to fill the bigger car twice, which was not only helpful but necessary since he found more items than he thought he would. His small car would have led to some tough decisions as to what to take and what to leave behind.

After Ethan's car was towed, the two men took off toward Ethan's hotel. They stopped to put gas in the car, and Ethan went into the little store to use the restroom and grab a coffee while Edward filled the tank. That was when he saw her . . . well, almost bumped into her would be more accurate. For a moment, it took his breath away. She looked just like Mrs. Parish but couldn't be . . . couldn't be . . . Mrs. Parish was gone. His brain went into overdrive. . . . Her daughter . . . her daughter . . . she was young when Mrs. Parish disappeared. He struggled to remember how old the girl was. Around ten? The girl standing before him, the girl he startled more than a bit . . . the girl he almost covered in piping-hot coffee . . . the girl standing before him had to be—just had to be—Mrs. Parish's daughter. She was the spitting image of Mrs. Parish. His heart sunk. She looked absolutely terrified of him.

Once again, Ethan wanted to turn around and return to Virginia. She couldn't know who he was . . . could she? She couldn't know that he was the boy whom many believed had something to do with her mom's disappearance. No way she could know, but why else would she look so rattled by the sight of him? After an awkward moment, even by his standards, he somehow got the words, "Sorry, you good?" out of his mouth. She responded with a nod of her head.

He paid for the coffee and left the store with his head down. *Such a beautiful girl.* She looked so much like her mother. That was one news story he had kept track of. He knew she was never found, and no arrest was ever made. Memories of Mrs. Parish always made him a little sad. She was one bright spot in Harperstown, her and his mom . . . both gone. But as he learned, Harperstown had a way of getting rid of good people. He would have liked to talk to her and let her know how sorry he was for her loss and how important her mom was in his life. More accurately, how she helped to save his life. He would love to share this information with her but knew that would never happen. The way she looked at him in the store reassured him that leaving those words unsaid was best for all involved.

Ethan was totally unaware that Edward, who was pumping gas, had a bird's-eye view of the encounter and couldn't help but notice how socially awkward Ethan still appeared. He also couldn't help but observe how beautiful the young girl was. The spitting image of her mother.

The rest of the weekend unfolded better than he thought it would, better than he had dared to hope. He swam his way through the painful memories. Dealing with Edward wasn't nearly as bad as he feared it would be. Edward proved to be helpful while giving him his space. Ethan was thankful for all the years of counseling he endured, and he finally felt like he was reaping the benefits.

The apex moment of healing occurred Sunday morning on his way back home. He took a minor detour to Woodlawn Cemetery, where he laid a beautiful, flowered wreath on the stone that read Mary Crow. He kneeled. With tears in his eyes, he said the words left unsaid for so many years. Ethan told his mom he was sorry for so many things. He told her all about his job, the house he was buying, and in between sobs, he asked her for forgiveness and told her how much she was loved. This was the memory running through his mind as he navigated the Beemer along the lakeside road back to Harperstown for the second time in as many weeks. This time, he would stay at Edward's house. He was certain this would be his last trip to Harperstown.

Seven

The evening that followed her birthday luncheon was full of activity, which helped to keep Katie's mind from obsessing about the day's eventful luncheon. She had agreed to help Ally out with a concert that was part of the college's annual Fall Fest celebration. With an extremely popular band headlining the event and the unseasonably warm weather, the turnout was larger than expected. Katie kept busy, lending a hand throughout the evening.

She was not blind to the fact that every time Ally sent her somewhere to help, she ended up working with the same person, a young man named Shane. Ally was not the most subtle of matchmakers, nor did she have bad taste. Shane was not only fun to work with, but he was also easy on the eyes. Katie could tell by the way he kept looking at her that the feeling was mutual, but she was not in a place to start a relationship now, especially with the nightmares and this psychic guy bringing memories of her mom and the puzzling nature of her disappearance front and center once again.

The puzzle that was with her most of her life left her unable to fully trust people and feel completely secure—and it left her with a fear of an impending disaster or abandonment that would leave her alone, all alone. She was friendly and enjoyed his company, but before it could go any further, she put the proverbial wall up—the wall that politely but effectively let people, in this case, Shane, know that she was not interested.

It wasn't until after midnight that the two friends were in the apartment at the same time.

"Howdy, stranger!" Ally greeted Katie with her usual enthusiasm.

"Aren't you tired?" Katie answered. "It was quite the busy day, to say the least."

"It sure was, and I haven't even been able to talk with you about any of it! Especially that Peter guy that showed up at your birthday lunch. Wow, now that was crazy!"

"I know," Katie said thoughtfully. "I am still spinning from that. At first, I thought it was a trick or something planned by you. I wasn't sure if he was going to pull out a crystal ball or break into a striptease." She chuckled.

"Ahhh! Come on, I could do without that image! Give me more credit than that, please. I would not send someone old enough to be your dad!" Both girls broke into a brief laugh. "But seriously, that was surreal."

"That's putting it mildly. I have had little time to process it all because somebody has kept me hopping all night. Would you be able to survive tomorrow without me?"

"It will be quite the challenge and not as much fun, but I will muddle through," Ally answered, displaying an exaggerated pout face. "What's up? Is everything okay?"

"Yeah, I guess. I just need to go home and spend some time with my dad and Patty. I am going to head out in the morning . . . that is, if you can handle things without me." She grinned at her friend.

"No sweat. Do what ya gotta do."

"Thanks," Katie replied while heading out of the room. "Oh, yeah, FYI, Shane and I did not hook up." With that, Katie closed the bathroom door and stepped into the shower. Before turning on the shower, she heard Ally mutter, "Damn!"

Her head didn't hit the pillow until after 1:30 a.m. She was awoken by a terrifying nightmare and found herself sitting straight-up in bed, fists clenched, trying desperately to catch her breath. The time on her cell phone reaffirmed what she already knew. It was 3:24.

Katie swung her legs over the side of the bed and grabbed the water bottle from her nightstand. Sipping the cold water, she struggled to gain her composure. *I must be going crazy*, she thought. Her mind began racing as she struggled desperately to make sense of everything—the nightmares, the panic attacks, and the constant knot in her stomach. And, as if that weren't enough, now there was this Peter guy.

That time—3:24—was the same time displayed on the clock on the dash of her car two weeks before when this all started. She remembered that afternoon vividly. Even in her rattled, panicked state leaving the store, she knew that could not possibly be the correct time. It was 12:15. She was sure of this because she had looked at the clock in the store to make sure she would not be late for her 12:30 appointment. When she got in her car, she instinctively looked at her dash clock and noted that the clock was reading 3:24. She promptly set the clock to match the time on her cell phone, 12:16.

That date and time was when this all started. Once again, she replayed the moment in her mind—the event that had occurred in the store and caused the onset of panic attacks coinciding with the nightmares. It wasn't a big event at all. Nothing out of the ordinary. She was heading to the coffee station when a man who had just filled up his cup turned abruptly and almost knocked into her. With quick reflexes, he raised the cup in the air, stepped backward, and avoided showering her with coffee.

Her reaction to the man was the unusual aspect of the encounter, her entire body was engulfed with fear. She felt a sense of panic she had never felt before. She was sure the man yielding the coffee cup noticed her reaction because he stared at her for a moment, looking almost scared. He was probably bracing himself for anger. After what seemed like an eternity, he said, "Sorry, you good?" Katie, in the throes of panic, stood speechless, but she managed to nod her head. Simply recalling the event made her feel uncomfortable, and she was not sure why.

Eight

—◆—

Unlike two weeks earlier, Ethan was enjoying this morning's ride to Harperstown. The rhythm of the tires on the road had a soothing effect on his nerves. He could not help but take in the beautiful scenery around him. Thankfully, the day had a slightly different feel to it than his previous visit a couple weeks earlier. He got on the road early, allowing for time to stop by his classroom to double-check the plans he left for the substitute teacher and make sure everything was in order. He didn't miss school often, mostly because he found it more difficult leaving sub plans than going to work feeling a bit under the weather. He knew full well that the substitute teacher would be a qualified teacher, but he had yet to get a certified art teacher as a sub, and today was no exception. Today's plans had the substitute showing a movie on the impressionist movement.

When he hit the road, things at school were in order, his house closing was on schedule, and he was excited about acquiring more items from his childhood for his new home. It was a pleasant surprise to discover that his taste was similar to his mother's. The sun was shining, the air was warm, and the red, orange, and yellow leaves painted a lovely landscape. He was feeling much more relaxed than on his first visit, which went much better than he expected. Despite that, he found it difficult to shake the feelings of nervousness and anxiety that arose in him when he was around Edward. He always felt anxious and nervous around him. Even though his last visit was not as bad as he feared and he did not feel as uncomfortable around Edward as he used to, he still found himself fighting off an anxiety that was rising within him.

It was at this point of the trip that he decided to put the many years of counseling to the test and utilize the various coping skills he learned. He made a conscious decision not to let the past control him. He knew he had to face the memories that haunted him all these years. Taking slow, deep breaths, he gained his composure while reminding himself that he was no longer the angry, awkward teenage boy he was back then. Facing his past, including Edward and Harperstown, going through his mom's belongings, and spending the weekend in that house instead of at a hotel was essential to healing and moving on with his life.

The decision to stay at the house was made easier because Edward was so helpful on his first visit. He could not muster up the degree of hatred he once had for him. He still felt anxious and nervous around him, but not angry or hateful. After all, his mom had loved him, and he must have loved her; he was bending over backward to help Ethan. He even held onto her car all these years. He not only held onto it but kept it in mint condition, which Ethan was grateful for.

Cruising down the road in his mom's old car helped Ethan maintain a positive frame of mind, making it easier to fight off the demons from his past. The comfortable ride of the Beemer combined with the beautiful weather—a sunny day with warm temperatures and endless blue skies—allowed Ethan to cruise down the road, windows and sunroof wide open, circulating unseasonably warm air throughout the car, making it almost impossible to be angry.

Nine

———•◆•———

Edward pulled the warm sheets from the dryer and made his way down the hall toward the guest bedroom. He was sure it was a good idea to put Ethan in the guest bedroom rather than his old bedroom. He was in an unusually good mood and found himself singing along to the Rolling Stones song blaring from his Bose speakers.

> *Pleased to meet you*
> *Hope you guessed my name, mm yeah*
> *But what's puzzling you*
> *Is the nature of . . .*

The ringing of his phone emanated through the speakers, putting an abrupt halt to the music. Edward fumbled with the remote but managed to turn down the volume before answering the phone.

"Hello."

"Morning, Edward, Joe here."

"Hey, Joe, what's the word?"

"I'm afraid it is not good. Engine seized up. It's shot, not even worth fixing. Sorry!"

"I expected that."

"Well, for what it's worth, I can take care of junking it for you, or for Ethan, that is."

"Okay, I will call him. He should be on his way now."

"Sounds good. Tell him he will get six hundred bucks for junking it."

"Will do! I'll get back to you after I talk to him."

"Talk to ya soon. Again, tell him sorry!"

As soon as he hung up from that call, he called Ethan and was pleasantly surprised that it did not go to voice mail like it usually did.

"Hello," Ethan said, sounding at ease.

"Hey, Ethan, it's Edward. Is this a good time?"

"Yep, just finished filling your car."

"That's why I'm calling. I just got the word on your car, and it's not good."

"I was afraid you were going to say that." Ethan sighed.

"Sorry to be the bearer of bad news, but the engine seized up. It will cost more than it's worth to fix it."

"Shit!"

"I know, but he said you will get six hundred dollars for junking it, and I would love it if you would take the Beemer now. We can transfer it over to you, or I could sell it and give you the money. Whatever you'd prefer."

"No . . . you don't need to do that!"

"I know I don't need to, but I'd like to. Did you wonder why I held on to it all these years? I was holding on to the hope that someday you'd change your mind and decide you wanted it. Please take it. I know it's what your mom would want."

Ethan could not argue with that, nor did he have another option. He thanked Edward and told him he would be arriving shortly, which gave them time to get things taken care of. While returning to his spot behind the wheel, he felt a warmth for Edward that caught him by surprise, as did the beautiful memories of his mom dancing in his brain.

Edward always loved it when a plan just came together on its own. All the pieces simply fall into place with little or no effort, as if the universe takes the wheel and does the work for you, graciously showing you the way. The plan continued to unfold perfectly. Ethan was actually going to stay at the house, not at a hotel. He would take ownership of his mother's old car and was not only taking his call but sounded upbeat and perhaps happy to hear from him. At the very least, his guard was down. He was not keeping him at arm's length. Things were definitely falling into place. With a zip in his step, he resumed his work, cranked up the music, grabbed the sheets from the laundry room, and headed into the guest bedroom to make up the bed. The music was echoing throughout the house.

Just as every cop is a criminal
And all the sinners saints
As heads is tails
Just call me Lucifer
'Cause I'm in need of some restraint

Ten

I was not typical for Patrick O'Malley—or simply O'Malley as almost everyone called him—to order a second martini at lunch, but then again, this was not a typical lunch. He was enjoying a special retirement lunch with his long-time friend, Carl. The get-together had both a nostalgic and celebratory feel to it. The two men repeatedly raised their drinks and clanked their glasses together. "To retirement . . . to sleeping in . . . to watching sports . . . to winters filled with warm temperatures, sunshine, fishing, and relaxation." All this toasting resulted in the need to order a third drink. Wisely, the men switched from martinis to beer. They could keep the drinks coming without worry, as they had both taken an Uber to the pub, and their wives would join them for dinner and serve as their ride home.

It was only fitting that the two men would raise their glasses and say goodbye to a career they both loved. They had trained together, and on many occasions over the years, they had opportunities to work together. Throughout the years, their wives had developed a strong friendship as well. Despite living an hour away from each other, the couples got together frequently for dinners, concerts, sporting events, and the occasional weekend at a nearby casino. It was only natural that O'Malley and Carl's first retirement trip would include the four of them. In five days, the four of them would be sitting on a beach in Maui.

Carl raised his half-full beer and said, "To Maui!"

"To Maui," O'Malley responded over the sound of clanging glasses.

In recent years, ten to be exact, O'Malley worked at the Genovive Falls Police Department and Carl was captain at South Lake Police Station, which was about seventy miles from the Genovive Falls station. Although they did not work together on a daily basis, they had ample opportunity to communicate and help each other out. Most of their work-related interactions were by phone, usually asking for information on a particular person or case or requesting the other to hang missing people bulletins up around town.

It was funny to think that the two men would be spending more time together in retirement than they had while working together. After their Maui trip, the couples would go their separate ways to enjoy the holiday season with family, but come January, they would join forces again and head to Florida to ride out the heart of winter together. They would stay in a three-bedroom condominium located on the Intracoastal Waterway. The rental included easy dock access and would be perfect for the twenty-seven-foot Ranger Tug Carl purchased months ago. The tug fit perfectly into their retirement plans since it was a towable, ocean-worthy boat. This would enable Carl to use it at home during the spring and summer season and bring it to Florida for the winter months. This year's plan was to take the boat out on day trips and some short overnight trips to check out different locations in Florida and choose where they would like to snowbird in the future.

"What's this Eileen tells me about you working the evening shift this weekend?" Carl asked.

"Well, it's festival weekend, and Lieutenant Jefferson called in a favor."

"If I was a real good friend, I would volunteer to help out this weekend, but . . ."

"You are not a really good friend?" O'Malley quipped.

"Ha-ha! I do have some things to take care of tomorrow."

Looking up, Carl saw his wife approaching the table.

"Take care of what tomorrow? A hangover, perhaps," his wife Eileen said. She smirked, leaning down to give him a kiss.

Eleven

The line at the DMV was exactly what one would expect on a Friday afternoon. Ethan took a seat in the hard plastic chair and looked at the paper in his hand. His number was seventy-eight. A quick glance up showed them serving customer fifty-six, which meant he would be waiting a while. They had already taken care of junking Ethan's old car, received payment and paperwork of the transaction, and collected all the paperwork needed to register the BMW in Ethan's name. Edward was quite thorough, checking online and making a follow-up call to ensure they had everything they needed. They filled out all the required paperwork at the house, so all they could do was sit and wait.

Sitting in the uncomfortable chair, Ethan found his thoughts drifting to the past once again. For the second time that day, he was surprised that he was overcome with happy memories with his mom; for years, the only memory he could muster up was the one of him sitting next to her lifeless body. But sitting here in the DMV, his mind drifted back to the day he got his permit. He was so happy that day; he couldn't be mean or quiet or miserable. His mom was so proud of him that she took him straight to a wide-open parking lot to give him a feel for the car. Once he felt comfortable, she let him drive them to a local restaurant where they enjoyed a wonderful dinner of his favorite version of surf and turf, crab legs and steak. He recalled his mom getting all emotional and gushing that she couldn't believe her little boy was old enough to drive a car. They had such a fun, carefree evening filled with easy conversation. The memory left him sad, sad that his teenage moods and anger didn't allow for many times like that with his mom. He desperately longed for more.

Because Edward's presence was not needed in the DMV, he went to the car to make some phone calls. He wanted to get the car looked over, have the oil changed, and rotate the tires before Ethan drove it home on Sunday. That meant he would have to find a place that could do it all within twenty-four hours. His good luck continued as the best mechanic in town had to stay open for an emergency repair. Because of the nature of the job, he would have to keep a few guys on, but for much of the evening, they would be left twiddling their thumbs. Suffice it to say, he did not like paying people to sit around.

"So, if you don't mind waiting a bit longer than usual, bring it in around five o'clock, and I will have my team work on it in when they are not needed on the emergency repair."

"That would be awesome! Thanks, Dave! I will see you tonight."

The auto repair shop was a solid forty minutes away, which worked out perfectly for Edward. He could drop Ethan off at the house, giving him time to pack the items he wanted, and Edward could head to the repair shop, spending less time alone with him. Feeling relieved and more than a little blessed, he hung up the phone. He was placing the phone in its car holder when Ethan texted that he was all set and on his way. As Ethan approached the car that he was officially the proud owner of, Edward stepped out of the car and tossed him the keys. "Your car now, so you do the driving."

Ethan, who was still battling with bouts of anxiety around Edward, was certain that he did not want to drive with Edward in the car. Mustering a smile, he responded, "Thanks, but if you wouldn't mind chauffeuring me one more time, I'd appreciate it. I'm exhausted."

Edward obliged willingly. Actually, he was more than a little relieved. He had always despised being a passenger, as he hated not being in control. On the drive home, Edward filled Ethan in on the car repair situation.

"That will give you some time to get things done without me in the way."

"You sure you don't want me to bring the car over? I mean, you have done so much for me already today."

"I'm sure. It makes sense, since you are the one with a lot to do at the house. I'll drop you off and head over to the shop."

The evening passed more quickly than Ethan thought it would. He made good use of the time Edward gave him and was able to go through the closets that contained a lot of his mom's items and her old art room. He was working in the art room when Edward returned home. He was sure he heard his car, but he had not entered the house yet. Puzzled, Ethan walked into the kitchen and found Edward entering the house. "Car's all set. You must be hungry."

"I hadn't thought about it. But now that you mention it, I'm starving!"

"There's a great Chinese place about fifteen minutes away. If I put an order in, would you mind taking your car to pick it up?"

"Not at all," Ethan replied.

◆ ◆ ◆

With his stomach growling in response to the delicious smells coming from the food bag beneath the passenger seat, Ethan maneuvered the car up the long driveway to Edward's house. The entire trip only took him a little over half an hour. Bag of food in hand, Ethan entered the house. "Dinner is served!" Ethan called out. He was met with silence. Quietly, Ethan went about setting the table. When he finished, he called out again. "Edward, I'm back with dinner." Again, he was met with silence.

Just as Ethan was going to try to locate Edward, the back door opened, and Edward entered the kitchen. Disheveled hair and rosy cheeks made him look windblown, prompting Ethan to ask if everything was okay.

"Everything is fine. I just had to do a few things at the boathouse. When the sun goes down, it sure gets chilly quick."

"Well, dinner is ready," Ethan replied.

"Good deal. I will wash up and be right there. Can I get you something to drink?"

"I will just have water, thanks."

With a full stomach, Ethan had little to no energy. He decided he'd be better off getting a good night's sleep and tackling everything else tomorrow. He grabbed his book off the coffee table and bid Edward a goodnight.

Twelve

John dropped Patty at her house, but not before questioning her about how she knew Peter. He recalled her initial reaction when she saw Peter at lunch, how she asked what he was doing there and knew to take notes while he talked. John hated the fact that he was questioning Patty, but the events of this afternoon had him more than a little rattled. He had moved past the shock and emotion of what Peter shared and returned to being suspicious. Patty's reaction to his interrogation revealed that she, too, was taken aback by Peter's presence at lunch. She told John how she heard a great deal about him and was told that he had an amazing gift. After Sharon disappeared, a good friend encouraged her to go and see him. When encouragement didn't work, her friend took it upon herself and got them tickets to see him at a local venue. She said, "I was skeptical, but I guess my desperation outweighed my skepticism because I accepted the offer and attended not one but two events." Patty continued, "It was interesting, to say the least. At the second event, I was positive he was going to do a reading on me. There was a point during the event when he paused and stared at me. My excitement rose, but he abruptly looked away. I was so disappointed! That was the last event of his I attended. As silly as it sounds, I was a little angry with him for not telling us what happened to Sharon, although I have heard a good deal about him over the years and know people who swear by him."

John listened intently and then proceeded to ask her questions about what information she gave prior to the event. He was desperately fishing, trying to uncover any connection Peter could have had to his family—to Patty or Sharon. She assured him they never had her name since, on both occasions, she was given a ticket purchased by a friend. "I never formally met him, and I never attended any other events that he was at." Her responses assured John that she was as in the dark as he was. Before she got out of the car at her house, he apologized for treating her like a suspect.

"No apology needed. Just get some sleep, and we will talk tomorrow."

"Okay, but if you think of anything that could shed some light on this whole thing, please give me a ring."

"Will do. You do the same."

He did not heed Patty's advice and found himself up well past midnight, scouring the computer for information on Peter. To his surprise, information was plentiful and extremely positive. He was revered as a great guy and a gifted psychic, not only by patrons but by the community. Even police around the country had put his skills to use on more than one occasion. They would call him in to give his thoughts and feelings on a case that had either stumped them or was an urgent matter. One of these cases involved a five-year-old autistic boy who had wandered away from his family's campground in a large national park. Peter's description of the boy's setting led rescuers to the scared boy in time to bring him home safe and sound. He was credited with helping to locate many missing persons and providing information that aided police in solving many cold cases.

Review after review, testimony after testimony, article after article—everything he read touted Peter's skills as a gifted psychic. They also praised him as a stand-up guy and valuable member of the community. There was one interesting article in which the investigative reporter tried to set him up so he could expose him as a fraud, but in the end, he abandoned the piece, opting instead to write about how the experience left him a believer. A year doesn't go by that he doesn't have a reading by Peter.

Try as he might, John could find nothing that portrayed him as a scam artist, nor could he find anything that would connect him to Sharon, Patty, Katie, or himself. Nothing. He could not think of a motive for him to want to crash into their life. When he sat down at the computer, he was certain he would find information that supported his hypothesis that Peter was a scam artist playing on people's emotions. He was expecting a call or another surprise visit from him, saying he had more information—crucial information that he would be happy to share with them. *For a small fee, of course!* he thought. But none of his online investigation gave any credence to this. He could not fathom any reason that he would have shown up like he did or had the information he had. No explanation at all made sense, other than the story Peter shared with them. *Sharon sent him, and he didn't have a clue why!*

Thirteen

The moon illuminated the otherwise dark room as he lay perfectly still on the bed, but his body was all that was still; his brain was working overtime. To say that his head was a busy place for the last two weeks would be an understatement. Busy but invigorating. With the time almost at hand, he was running a checklist through his mind.

Over the years, he learned that preparation, patience, and planning were all key components. As important as these three elements were, he recently became aware of the importance of remaining opportunistic, alert enough to seize an opportunity when it presented itself. God knows he had done that on more than one occasion.

His mind slipped back in time to two weeks earlier, when a surprise encounter did exactly that . . . presented him with an opportunity, an opportunity he simply could not pass up. As soon as he saw her, the Parish girl, all grown up and the spitting image of her mom, Sharon Parish, he knew this was his opportunity to get it right and finish the story. It was time to finish the book he started years ago, to finish and move on. He felt this in his bones, without a doubt. This was fate. This was his destiny. All of their destinies.

This was apparent in the way everything was falling into place as if it was meant to be. This was not just another chapter. No . . . this was the final chapter, the end of a story. All loose ends tied up. Every question answered. It was time to move on, time for a new story with new characters, a new setting, new victims, and, of course, a new villain. One thing life had taught him was that moving on to the new was impossible until the old was completely and thoroughly taken care of, which was exactly what he intended to do. And what a poetic ending it would be.

He adjusted his head slightly, just enough to get a glimpse of the box he had just placed on the desk next to his bed. Seeing the box triggered an emotional response in him. As good as he was at keeping emotions at bay, the box caused a lump to rise in his throat. His voice was barely audible as he whispered to himself, or perhaps to her, "Why did you have to be so nosey and go through the box when you discovered it? Why?"

Earlier in the evening, he had spent hours going through the contents of the box, which only reassured him that once she had seen its contents, she left him with no choice. She made the choice—a fatal choice! All he could do was respond, and respond he did, quickly, efficiently, and permanently. Even now, all these years later, he couldn't help but admire his quick thinking, action, and adaptability. In a matter of moments, she was gone. Gone forever and gone in a manner that would result in no questions being asked. Slowly and methodically, he went through each photo one by one, studying each one and memorizing every detail. He knew that after Sunday, he would never see the photos again. Although it was a necessary component of his plan, it still made him sad. After all these years, it amazed him that a simple shoebox could hold so much beauty!

Saturday

---◆---

OCTOBER 23, 2017

Fourteen

Inside the beautiful colonial house, John, who had given up on sleep hours ago, gazed out the window, oblivious to the breathtaking scene on the other side of the glass pane. Brilliant red, orange, and yellow leaves framed the yard, partially covered with dead leaves. The sun was rising, and the sky appeared to be painted a magnificent shade of blue. It was the type of morning that made the forthcoming winter bearable. Even with every window in the house closed, the honking sounds of geese escaping the impending cold could be heard.

The cream-colored home gave the illusion of being in the middle of nowhere, even though it was a five-minute drive into town and an easy ten-minute trip to the lake. The large lot contributed to the residents' feeling of isolation, being the only humans within miles. Sharon loved the feeling of being so far away from other people even though she wasn't. Mr. and Mrs. Jones were a mere two hundred yards to the right, just beyond the thick row of pine trees. The Fisher family resided to the left, in a sprawling ranch-style home, approximately a football field away.

Staring at a squirrel that was running from tree to tree, John could not stop thinking about Katie's birthday lunch. Questions were swirling around in his head. *Who is this guy? How did he find them? How did he know the things he knew?* It was the last question that unsettled him the most. How could he know she referred to him as George? Nobody knew that; nobody, except for him, Sharon, and perhaps Patty.

Last night's research failed to provide him with answers to his many questions. In fact, it left him more stumped and confused.

If he didn't buy into this psychic mumbo jumbo, which he did not, the only explanations he could think of were that this Peter knew Sharon, not just casually, and he had something to do with her disappearance. It was this thought that sent waves of terror through his entire body, but every instinct told him that was not the case. Sharon would never have been unfaithful to him in any way, shape, or form. Then there was the fact that he liked the man and had an unexplainable feeling of trust toward him.

He gazed down at the notes in his hands. Ally provided them to everyone after she charmed the manager of the restaurant into making copies of them. Referencing them now was completely unnecessary, as he had memorized every word that was written on the paper. He found himself completely baffled by one statement that Sharon supposedly told Peter. "You need to go through my memories. You need to share them with Katie." How could he possibly go through her memories? He said out loud to himself, "That Peter fellow will probably tell me he can get in touch with her memories, and, for a small fee, he will share them with me." He did not get the last word out when he felt his heart skip a beat. *Oh, my God, her memories!*

He stood frozen for a second and then quickly headed for the basement stairs. Taking the steps two at a time nearly resulted in him tumbling his way to the bottom. After fifteen minutes that felt like an eternity, he stared at the item he was desperately searching for. Directly in front of him, on the shelf, there was a box. On the front, written in Sharon's handwriting, were the words *MY MEMORIES*.

The dusty box was larger and heavier than he remembered. He struggled carrying the heavy box up from the basement. When he set it on the dining room table, the words, *MY MEMORIES*, written with a sharpie on the side of the box, seemed to scream out to him. In his mind, he replayed the words, *You need to go through my memories. You need to share them with Katie.*

Looking at the box, he felt sadness, loss, and confusion consume his entire body. How was he going to manage delving into its contents? He had spent years not just avoiding it but hiding from it. He reached for a can of Coke, or as Sharon used to call it, his "can of caffeine." She found it amusing that instead of a cup of coffee, he began each day with a can of warm coke. Slowly, he opened the box. The top layer was a mess of loose pictures, cards, and notes from the time Sharon went missing. He threw those items onto the table. With the stuff he had thrown into the box out of the way, he could see Sharon's much more organized collection of memories.

Seeing their wedding photos, followed by Katie's baby book, sparked many long-forgotten memories. In his mind, he could clearly see the day they brought Katie home from the hospital. John had taken a few weeks off work to help with Katie and get things settled in their home. He enjoyed being home all the time, basking in the luxury of being in the same town as his wife and baby girl. He knew things would return to normal in only a few short weeks. Well, normal for them. That would mean John leaving on Monday morning for work and returning on Friday evening.

Many of the people around town found this arrangement strange and felt that it meant they did not have a happy marriage. People loved to express their opinions in Harperstown—not usually to the person whom the opinion regarded, but to anyone else who would listen. The view many of the townspeople had of their unique living arrangement most definitely fueled the flames of suspicion that John was responsible for Sharon's disappearance. Of course, this was the talk among acquaintances and total strangers. For those who knew them well, this was mere gossip and speculation.

Their friends and family were certain that nothing could be farther from the truth. They were an extremely happy family, and they made the arrangement work. Being separated during the week had its struggles and drawbacks, but it also had its advantages. John worked long, hard hours during the week, but when he came home on Fridays, he left his work and the stress that accompanied it in the city. When he got home, it was truly family time. During the week, Sharon enjoyed spending an abundance of quality time with her daughter. With only her and Katie around, she managed to get plenty of sleep. She even found time to read, teach an after-school art class, and work on her paintings.

It is amazing how many memories one box can hold. With each item he pulled from the box, the story of a lifetime unfolded. He set a few photo albums aside because he did not have the emotional strength to go through them. The table that was now home to the contents of the box was no longer suitable for dining. One picture that made its way to the top of the pile was a photograph of Sharon when she was around Katie's age. The picture caught his eye, and he lifted it from the table to take a closer look. It was like looking at a picture of Katie! He was so mesmerized by the photo that he did not hear the door open or the approaching footsteps.

"Good morning, Dad." Katie's greeting startled him. She thought about phoning her father to let him know she was on her way but decided it would be best to surprise him. Over the years, she developed the habit of surprising him whenever the opportunity presented itself. She began using the surprise tactic as a test, maybe to catch him doing something, anything that screamed he knew something or was somehow involved in the disappearance of her mother. That may have been the origin of her habit of surprising him, but now it was simply a part of their relationship. She loved the look on his face when she showed up unexpectedly.

"What are you doing here?" He smiled as he made his way toward his only daughter.

"I came to see you. Is that a picture of me?"

"Nope . . . that's a picture of your mom at your age." He smiled.

"That could be . . . oh, my God . . . it looks just like me!" Katie stammered.

"It does indeed!"

"Whatcha got going on here?" she asked, pointing to the box. As she walked closer to the table, she read the writing on the box aloud. "My memories." She stared at the box for a moment and then asked in a weak voice, "Was that Mom's box?"

John nodded. "I was just emptying it and gathering the courage to go through it, as your mom requested."

"Oh, my God, it says, *MY MEMORIES.*" Katie began digging through her purse. With a slightly shaking hand, she pulled out her copy of the notes Ally took at lunch. Katie scanned the paper and then read aloud, "You need to go through my memories. You need to share them with Katie." She looked at her father as she said, "I do believe she wants us to do this together."

"I believe you are right." He took her hand in his. "Are you ready for this?"

A feeling of strength and hope engulfed her as she responded with a powerful voice, "I am way past ready."

Fifteen

Within an hour, the top of the solid oak table was no longer visible. They decided to empty the entire contents of the box before ciphering through it, which resulted in the table being covered with piles of loose photos, a couple of photo albums, and a few sketch pads. The walk down memory lane was an overdue emotional journey. Patty, who joined them shortly after the process began, had the foresight to come armed with a box of tissues.

Hours flew by as they released memory after memory from their cardboard hiding place. The result was a rush of emotions surging over John, like flooding waters when a dam breaks. Although he was standing in his dining room, in his mind, he was lost in days gone by, hiking the trails along the waterfalls with Sharon and Katie. He could see the sun's rays glistening like diamonds off the lake. He could hear the sounds of cascading water fill the air and the sound of ducks quacking expectantly as tiny Katie tossed breadcrumbs into the air. The memory was so powerful . . . so real. It was as if he was living the moment again. He could even hear Sharon's giggle of delight as she watched her little girl jubilantly telling the ducks to "share niceweee."

He had not felt this kind of connection with Sharon and the life they shared since the night she vanished into thin air. Gradually returning to reality, he looked toward the sky and mumbled to himself, "Oh, Sharon, I wish you were here now. I wish you were here with me." A chill ran up his spine as he felt a warm embrace around him.

"Can I get you something to drink?" Patty's words broke the silence that had filled the room.

"Umm . . . what?" John responded to the words that had abruptly pulled him from his journey to the past.

"Drink. Can I get you a drink?"

"Sure, I'll have a . . ."

"Coke." Patty completed his sentence with a chuckle.

"Just water for me," Katie chimed in.

While handing out the requested beverages, Patty said, "So, what are your thoughts on this Peter guy? I mean, some of the stuff he knew, like that, 'go through my memories' statement." Pointing to the box, she said, "Makes one wonder."

"That it does!" John replied. "Since I don't believe in all this psychic rigmarole, I have been racking my brain trying to make sense of it all."

"And?" Katie asked anxiously.

Not wanting to upset his daughter, John paused for a moment and weighed his words before answering. "I got nothing." He shook his head.

"Dad . . . stop trying to protect me. Peter came to me. We need to talk about this. I want . . . no, I *need* to know what you think!" Katie's voice quivered.

"Honey, I really don't know what to think."

"Are you staying for the weekend?" Patty asked Katie.

"I am staying tonight. I am planning on heading out in the morning to help Ally with the last day of the festival." Katie turned her gaze toward her father as she continued, "Which leaves us plenty of time to discuss Peter showing up in our lives."

Before she knew it, the questions from her father seemed to come fast and furious. It was as if he had morphed into a detective with a good deal of knowledge on psychic scams and techniques. It was during her dad's barrage of questions that

Katie blurted out, "I want to talk to him again. I want to hear what else, Mom . . . I mean, *he* has to say."

"I know you do, honey, but you know I don't believe in that psychic nonsense."

"Well then, how did he know everything? My birthday . . . my clock . . . communicating on the computer . . . the memory box?"

"Get a life, sista," Patty added as soon as Katie was finished talking.

"I don't know. I've been up most of the night trying to figure it out. I checked this Peter guy out on the computer, and well . . . I got nothing. I am baffled. If it's a scam, then he is pretty darn good at it!"

"Well, then, let's meet with him again," Katie suggested.

"I don't know if that's a good idea."

"What harm can it do?" Katie implored.

"It could bring up painful memories . . . give us false hope." John sounded a bit shaken.

"It brought up memories today." Katie waved her arm toward the dining room table. "Wonderful memories! Happy memories! And what hope? As he said, if she is communicating with him, then she is dead. Maybe we will get closure . . . answers . . . peace." Katie looked her dad directly in the eyes. "Please, Dad, please!" To John, she sounded twelve again.

"Okay, we will call him and set something up," John conceded.

"I'm on it." Patty smirked as she picked up her cell phone.

Sixteen

The small, ornately decorated living room was nearing full capacity. The recliners, couch, and love seat were occupied, along with half a dozen chairs from the kitchen. Thrown into the mix of fine furniture were several folding chairs, which, judging by their design, were locked in a closet for years. Making a quick assessment of the room, Peter noted that there were twenty people, twenty women, to be precise. He was approached by the hostess of the morning's event, known to him simply as Mrs. K. His assistant, Marlee, took care of everything else prior to the event. "Everyone's here, Mr. Dorjen, so you may begin whenever you are ready. Can I get you anything?" Mrs. K asked excitedly.

"Thank you. Water would be great."

Peter took the glass of ice-cold water and sat down in a comfortable chair that was facing the circle of chairs filled with women anxiously waiting to hear the words he would speak. Being such a small event, he took over Marlee's role of explaining how this worked and gave her a well-deserved day off. He suggested that everyone have paper and something to write with so that if the person next to them was given a reading, they could take notes for them. Then he explained he would try to read everyone, but there were no guarantees, and he informed the crowd that he did not follow any particular order.

He was grateful that the pang of nausea and uneasiness he felt in the car on the way to the event had subsided. It had come on suddenly and didn't last too long, and although it was short-lived, it was most definitely intense. Thankfully, it had passed with no lingering effects. He did readings on various guests. It did not take long for him to get in the groove. He was definitely in "the zone," as his mom liked to call it. The readings revolved around health issues, family problems, and the loss of loved ones. Some readings were long and involved, eliciting an emotional response from the person on the receiving end of the reading. Other readings were very brief and quite simple. Overall, it appeared to be a remarkably blessed group of women. Toward the end of the event, a few of the husbands, who were hanging out in the man-cave area of the basement, found their way upstairs. They were lucky enough to receive a reading from Peter, who was basking in the joy of participating in the routine of a planned event. However, Mrs. K's husband Steve probably did not feel that lucky when Peter did a reading on him. During the reading, Peter referenced romantic evenings, and judging by the look on both of their faces, these evenings did not involve Mrs. K. Of course, Peter had a feeling that this was the case before he spoke and said nothing accusatory or that would give him away, but he made sure to make him sweat a little and perhaps said enough to keep Mrs. K on her toes.

It was while he was doing a reading on one of the men that Peter felt distracted. It began with the image of the broken heart drawing, flashing repeatedly, followed by the hourglass. Then it was as if Sharon was next to him, tugging on his shirt, encouraging him to hurry and get out of there, which is exactly what he did.

On the ride home, Peter felt ill again. He noted it was in the same spot that he felt sick on the way to the event. It was on a stretch of the road that ran along the lake. Due to it being fall, Peter could catch glimpses of the lake through the partially leafed trees. Out of the blue, he was hit with a sudden wave of nausea, followed by a dizzy feeling, and then a moment or two when he found it difficult to get air. *Okay, since when do I get carsick?* he thought. Just as it had on the way to the event, the feeling passed quickly. Right before it completely subsided, shouts in Sharon's voice filled his head. "Couldn't save myself! Must save her!"

The ringing of his phone startled Peter and quickly brought him back to reality. The news delivered by the voice on the other end was the last thing he expected.

"Peter, this is Marlee." Peter heard the tears in her voice.

"Marlee, what's wrong? Are you okay?" He knew his words sounded panicked.

"No, I'm not. My mom has suffered a major stroke. It doesn't look good. Frank and I are flying out as soon as possible to see her. I don't know how long we will be gone. I am so sorry!"

"I am so sorry to hear that. Let me know if there is anything I can do. Don't worry about a thing here," Peter said softly but empathically.

She promised to keep in touch, and Peter promised to keep them in his prayers. When he hung up the phone, the reality that Marlee was gone struck him. He couldn't remember doing his job without her.

The sun was shining brightly, and he knew, although he would have to dress warmly as the temperatures plummeted later in the day, that even with a little side stop, he would have some time to kayak this evening. He didn't get out this way often, and he read that there was a new winery off this road. It had gotten rave reviews, so he took a minor detour and checked it out for himself.

One hour later, he was back on the road with his wallet a little lighter and his wine collection a bit fuller. Once again, the ringing of his phone broke the silence.

"You would think I'd see that coming," he mumbled. "Hello."

"Mr. Dorjen?" the vaguely familiar voice asked.

"Why, yes, it is. May I ask who is calling?"

"It is Patty. Sharon's Patty, from lunch yesterday."

"Yes, Patty, what can I help you with?"

"I was wondering if you had some time to meet with us? John, Katie, and me? We would really like to talk to you. We will pay you your normal fee." As she was speaking, he saw the image of an hourglass next to a puzzle that was missing pieces. He felt a sense of urgency rising. "Yes! I am free for the rest of the day." The words leapt off his lips before he had time to think about what he was saying. *So much for kayaking!*

Seventeen

Sitting across the room from Patty, Peter was still baffled by what he didn't see. No colors, no images, nothing. It was quite unnerving, as it was not normal for him to be with someone and not get a glimpse into their life, or at least their moods. Feeling rattled, he invited Patty to uncork the bottle of red wine he brought them. He took a long, slow sip to gather himself.

It wasn't just Patty that had him feeling unnerved. As soon as he began walking down the stone walkway to John's house, he felt Sharon's presence. He could feel her panic and was filled with a sense of danger during the walk to the front door. There was a new image, that of a white hanky flashing in his head. Thankfully, the feeling of danger and panic subsided the moment he entered the house. Peter joined John, Patty, and Katie as they took a seat in the living room. The warm weather alleviated the need for a fire, but Peter could not help but think of how warm and cozy this room would be with a roaring fire emanating from the granite fireplace. His senses kicked into overdrive upon entering their home. He was filled with a plethora of emotions that included love, laughter, joy, and even hope. As he glanced around the room, these feelings almost overtook him.

"Are you okay?" Patty's question brought Peter back to the here and now.

"I'm fine. Just admiring your beautiful home," Peter lied.

"Not mine," Patty said with a chuckle. "My home is closer to town and pales in comparison."

As usual, Sharon took over and dictated how things were to go. Peter was suddenly bombarded with images and thoughts that were not his. The painting of a broken heart, a puzzle with a missing piece, the numbers three, two, and four, the white hanky, and the initials EC.

"I believe Sharon is telling me she knows you are brokenhearted." Peter paused a moment before continuing, "Do the numbers three, two, and four mean anything to you? A birthday or an anniversary, perhaps?"

John and Patty answered in unison, "No, nothing I can think of."

"It means something to me," Katie said in a weak voice. "I have been having nightmares lately, and I wake up terrified every night at 3:24."

"How long has this been going on?" John inquired, painfully aware of how pale and frightened she looked.

"It's been a couple of weeks now. . . . Actually, it started two weeks ago yesterday."

"And you have had them every night since?" John quizzed his daughter.

"Unfortunately, yes, every night, and every night I awake at exactly 3:24. I have also been thinking of Mom a lot, and I've been experiencing some sort of . . . I don't know . . . strange feelings, like panic attacks."

"Why didn't you tell us?" John and Patty both asked.

"I don't know. I didn't want you to worry or make a big deal out of it."

Peter, who was listening intently, had one question for Katie. "Do you recall when the strange feelings started?"

"Yeah, it was the same day as the nightmares. Last Friday . . . around lunchtime."

Peter said the word *lunchtime* in perfect timing with Katie. Katie looked at him curiously.

"That is when I first felt Sharon's presence." Peter's words seemed to hang in the room.

"And you are sure that was when this all began?" her dad inquired.

"Absolutely!" Katie shared the story of the man with the coffee, her reaction, and the time on the clocks. "The funny thing is he seemed like a normal guy, nothing freaky about him, nothing that should have caused me to feel fearful and panicked. Yet . . . I did. I felt . . . well . . . I feared for my life."

Not knowing what else to say, Peter said, "Trust your gut. It is always wise to trust your gut."

"I have to agree with that," Patty said.

"God knows I listen to mine," he said as he tried to force a smile and appear calm, which was extremely difficult with the image of an hourglass with the sands running out repeatedly flashing in his head.

Eighteen

Lying in bed, O'Malley was extremely grateful that he did his lieutenant a favor by agreeing to work the three to eleven shift for the next two days. With the college festival in full swing, there was no question it was where he was most needed, and he was happy to help one last time. Spending his last two days working a different shift allowed him to get the emotional goodbyes with his closest colleagues out of the way. An added bonus to working the evening shift was that he did not have to be up early for work. He took full advantage of this, and by the time he opened his eyes, the sun was up and shining through his bedroom window. He immediately regretted the last couple of drinks he had the night before. With a slight groan, he rolled over and reached out to give Carol, his wife of thirty-six years, a hug, but he only found crumpled blankets. Struggling to focus on the clock made his head hurt even more.

"Hey there, sleepyhead," Carol said.

"What time is it?"

"It is 9:30," Carol replied while handing her husband a glass of water and two aspirins. "This should help get you up and moving. Coffee is ready when you are."

He took the pills and, after swallowing them, handed Carol the glass and managed a smile. "You're the best."

"Don't you forget it!" Carol chuckled while heading out of the room.

There was more truth in those words than she would ever know. He couldn't even imagine life without his amazing wife and hoped he'd never have to. He knew being a cop's wife was not easy. She had spent more time worrying about him and his safety than he could ever imagine. He felt her relief of those days being behind them when he told her he'd be filling in for the lieutenant, working the desk rather than the streets for his last two shifts. For her, the worrying was a thing of the past, and before she knew it, they would be basking in the Maui sun.

O'Malley felt better quicker than he thought he would and actually looked halfway human when he arrived at work. Even though it was not his usual shift, or group of officers, for that matter, he fell comfortably into the role of lieutenant for the night. He had worked with most of the men from time to time, just not on a regular basis. One thing working in law enforcement for over thirty-three years had taught him was how to adapt to all situations, so he was not surprised at how smoothly things were going. *Probably just the calm before the storm,* he thought as he stepped out of his temporary office to grab a cup of coffee. As he turned down the hallway, he was surprised to see his good friend Carl talking with the officer at the front desk.

"Did you have a sudden attack of conscience and come to lend me a hand?" O'Malley teased.

"Not exactly. I have a favor to ask of you."

"Sure thing, come on in," O'Malley said while waving his hand toward his office door. The look on Carl's face told him this was not a joking matter.

As soon as the two men were in the office, O'Malley said, "What's up?"

"Last night, a teenage girl went missing. We are friends with her parents. They go to our church, and Eileen has done a lot of volunteer work and committees with her mom. Understandably, her parents are a wreck. Since I'm no longer on the force, I am struggling to help anyway I can."

"Understandable. What you got?"

"Well, her name is Beth. She is seventeen years old. Friday night outside of the football game, she had a fight with her boyfriend and stormed off. She hasn't been seen since then."

"And the boyfriend?"

"He checks out. He was with her friends as they went looking for her. They looked for a few hours before letting her parents know. From that point, he has been with either her family or his. No other suspects, but the police found her book bag with a few items in it, including her wallet and some cash. There was one strange thing found inside it, a drawing. On the front, there is a broken heart, and on the back, written in jagged lettering, is the word *BROKENHEARTED*. Nobody has seen it before. Not her parents, friends, or boyfriend. They say she is not artistic at all. Her mom is insistent that it is a clue." Carl handed Patrick a copy of a missing person flier. It had a picture of Beth as well as a picture of the broken heart picture found in her book bag.

"Where was the bag found?"

"In the grass just off of Lake Road, about a twenty-minute walk from the football field."

"We will get these out in the community. I will also make sure all the guys are aware of the situation and that they keep an eye out for her. There is a lot of activity here this weekend with the festival in full swing."

"Thanks, I appreciate it. I'm not used to feeling so helpless when things like this happen."

"I can only imagine. Well, for a couple of more days at least!"

Nineteen

The hourglass flashing in his mind slowly faded, and Peter felt a strange calm come over him. It was as if Sharon's thoughts and feelings were vivid in his mind now. "I have a powerful feeling that Sharon is with me. She wants me to listen to her, and, as I have said before, she is very persistent!" His remark elicited a chuckle from the room. "I believe she has some messages for all of you."

With that comment, Peter gave detailed descriptions of days past. It seemed as if there was a memory that would convince each one of them that this was most definitely Sharon talking. Peter felt her desperation for them to believe, without a doubt, that it was her.

For Patty, she referenced items that left Peter baffled but obviously struck a chord with Patty. "I am seeing a woman in labor, but she is holding a golf club." Peter had an amused but puzzled look on his face.

"Oh, my God!" Patty mumbled, "I'd rather be golfing." Those were the words Sharon yelled as she was getting ready to deliver Katie. Of course, she went into labor unexpectedly, and John was trying desperately to get there in time, but it was Patty and Sharon alone until right before she delivered their baby girl.

Feeling a need to look at and speak to John, Peter looked directly at him and said, "I see a little girl, about two years old, feeding bread to a gaggle of ducks; they are all around her, and she is so happy."

John felt his head spin but managed to get the words out of his mouth. "That is the exact scene I was remembering while looking through the box this morning," he said in a hushed tone.

Katie could tell by the looks on her dad's and Patty's faces that Peter's words meant something. She felt a rising anticipation when Peter turned to her. "I am seeing a collage of pictures moving fast. It is almost like the old picture books; you know, the ones you flip so quickly that it plays like a movie. I see a young girl. She is looking around the house. She is looking for someone. Her mom, she is looking for her mom. She picks up the phone. Then she keeps looking. On her way through the kitchen, she picks up an apple, not to eat. . . . She is holding it like a baseball, like a weapon." Peter stopped talking as the flip-book came to an abrupt end.

A tear rolled down Katie's cheek. Peter had just described her movements and actions on the morning she discovered her mother was missing. He described everything; he even mentioned the apple.

Seeing the tear on her face and the pain in her eyes, John took on the role of protective father. "Okay, I think we have had enough. This is too upsetting for Katie. You heard her say she has been having troubles . . ."

Katie quickly cut her father off. "Oh, no . . . not upsetting me at all. All these years, I felt abandoned and alone. I often wondered if Mom just left. . . . She . . . she didn't leave me! She was with me that morning. Maybe not physically, but she was with me, watching over me."

"I know how you feel, honey, but it is emotionally overwhelming just the same," John responded.

Peter hadn't noticed while he was delivering messages, but he realized that Patty had written notes on everything he had said. "Did you take notes while I was talking?"

"Sure did."

"What about when I was talking to you?"

"Well, I had John take them then."

"Sure did!" John replied.

Peter felt Sharon's extremely strong presence once again. It was accompanied by flashes of Patty and him at one of his reading events. She was with him, sitting in the passenger seat of his car as he drove. This image reminded him of Marlee and her need to be away. The voice in his head, the voice of Sharon, was yelling, *"Ask her! Ask her! Ask her!"* After a week, Peter was aware of Sharon's persistence when she wanted him to do something, so he turned to Patty and asked if she knew anyone who could fill in as his assistant. He explained that his assistant had a family emergency and would be out of town for a while.

"I know the perfect person!" Katie exclaimed. "Aunt Patty."

A mere five minutes later, the decision was made. With years working as an administrative assistant at hospitals and schools, Patty, who had recently retired, would be the perfect person for the job. Peter was not oblivious to how happy this made Katie and John. He could see it in the colors surrounding them, although his inability to read Patty meant he would have to take her at her word.

After Patty agreed to fill in as his assistant, Peter excused himself to use the bathroom. On his way there, he walked past Katie and was immediately bombarded with the familiar images of an emptying hourglass, a puzzle with a missing piece, the numbers three, two, and four, and the broken heart painting, but now they were accompanied by Sharon screaming, *"Must save her! Save her! Please! Help her!"* These words he kept to himself.

Twenty

The day was more productive than Ethan dared to hope. Before the sunset, he glanced around the room in amazement. Not only had he gone through everything he wanted to, but he had also packed the items he wanted into bags and boxes, and with Edward's help, the car was ready for the road—all checked out, oil changed, and the tires rotated. The only task awaiting him was fitting everything into the Beemer, which he figured he could do in the morning, Ethan told Edward that he wanted to treat him to dinner to thank him for his hospitality. When Edward objected, Ethan made it clear that he would not accept no for an answer.

"Okay, I'll let you take me out to dinner, but I am treating us to an Uber. We have both earned a cold one, or perhaps two." Edward chuckled. It didn't take long for Ethan to agree and for the two men to settle on Baileys, a small Irish tavern known for its delicious burgers. This choice of restaurant made Ethan happy because it was a place he had never been with his mom, so it shouldn't trigger any memories. He swam through enough memories for a weekend and didn't feel like dealing with anymore even, or maybe especially, if they were good.

The restaurant was popular, so they were not surprised that they would have to wait forty minutes or so to get a table. However, they were pleasantly surprised that two seats at the bar opened as they were approaching. They gladly took the seats, ordered their drinks, and began watching a hockey game. The New York Rangers were playing the Boston Bruins. Ethan always enjoyed watching hockey, even though he never played it. He skated a bit when he was younger. His mom loved to skate and used to take him frequently, especially around Thanksgiving and Christmas. As he grew older and more disagreeable, he refused to go with her. He never did skate with her here in Harperstown. *Damn! I was sure that at this unfamiliar restaurant, I'd be safe from memories creeping up on me!* he thought to himself while pushing the memory down to the dark recess where it came from.

The noise at the bar was not obnoxious, but it was enough to keep the conversation at a minimum. This worked perfectly for Ethan, as he wasn't forced to make small talk with Edward. He couldn't help but notice the table behind him. It was comprised of two couples who, judging by the amount of laughter, were truly enjoying their night out. It did not take Ethan long to figure out that they were celebrating one of the couple's engagements. He shifted his position on the barstool, allowing him to view the source of the celebration. He did not need to see the ring the girl proudly displayed to her friend on the other side of the table to know that she was the one they were celebrating. The sparkle in her eyes rivaled the sparkle of the diamond.

Ethan found himself riveted to the group behind him. Although he appeared to be watching the hockey game, he had no clue what was going on. He couldn't tell anyone the score if asked, but thanks to his teacher's astute sense of hearing, he was able to listen to the conversation and take in the joy that was emanating from the table. They were clearly longtime friends with a strong connection to each other, a friendship Ethan had never known. He found it difficult to relate to people and nurture close relationships. In fact, the closest he got to this type of friendship was moments like this, moments when he could watch and partake in other people's happiness in his own mind. However, recently, he had begun to feel his own moments of happiness, his own pride, and even though he did not have any real close friends—or a girlfriend—he had work acquaintances and a handful of what he considered buddies. He also had his art, not to mention he was soon to be a homeowner. Wow, he was most definitely adulting.

Ethan noticed that as the foursome was preparing to leave. One of the men stood directly behind him, and Ethan heard him tell the server that the next hundred dollars of drinks ordered at the bar were on him. Once again, he was thankful for his teacher's sense of hearing. He waved the bartender over and ordered another round for him and Edward. From his seat at the bar, he lifted his glass to his lips and drank to the future.

Twenty-One

Patty hung around the house for a little while after Peter left, but when John and Katie invited her to join them out for dinner, she graciously declined their offer. She was getting bombarded with emails from Marlee, who was sending her information to prepare her for their upcoming phone conversation. Marlee would call Patty later in the evening to finish preparing her and to answer questions she may have. The number of emails Marlee sent to Patty heightened both her curiosity and her anxiety. In order to have adequate time to prepare for their phone conference, she headed home earlier than she planned. With the plethora of emails that continued to fill her inbox, Patty was sure she would need every minute.

After almost two hours of working at her computer, Patty felt much less anxious and far more excited. She had a list of questions to ask Marlee when she called. The darkness that loomed outside her office window reaffirmed that evening had arrived. Judging by Marlee's meticulous records, she was sure her phone would ring anytime now. She stood up, stretched her legs, opened the cupboard, retrieved a lemon ginger tea bag, and brewed herself a cup. As if on cue, the phone rang as soon as she returned to the seat at her desk.

"May I speak to Patty, please?"

"This is Patty."

"Well, hello. I'm Marlee. Is this a good time for you?"

"Absolutely! I just finished going through all the stuff you sent me."

"And I am sure you are feeling a wee bit overwhelmed."

Marlee chuckled. "I can't thank you enough for taking over for me like this."

"Oh, no problem. I hope your mom is doing well. I'm glad I can be of help, and just for the record, I find the whole thing intriguing and more than a little fascinating."

Marlee cleared her throat and seemed to hesitate before she said, "I don't mean to overstep my bounds, but how do you and Peter know each other?" Patty gave Marlee the abridged version of the story, and Marlee seemed to hang on to every word. "That explains so much about his behavior the past couple of weeks," Marlee said as much to herself as to Patty.

"You mean he didn't tell you any of this?"

"Nope, it's news to me. He told me to reschedule some events and to leave his calendar open for the next few weeks, except for a handful of events that he said he felt he must do. That is why the schedule for upcoming events is pretty sparse, which will be good for you to get your feet under you. With any luck, I will be back before things get crazy again."

The two talked for over an hour. Marlee guided Patty through the booking process for readings and events. Peter didn't want to be given any information beforehand, no names, no addresses, absolutely nothing that would lead to speculation that he Googles people for information. She explained to Patty that when booking an event, she was to get the number of people attending, not the names, and take credit card payments over the phone or they could pay in check or cash prior to the event. Then she would take down the address of the event. The only information she was to put on Peter's calendar was the time and how far away it was. It was her job to put the event addresses into Peter's GPS, or if that was not possible, she could text him the address as he was leaving. Patty was stunned at the efforts the two went through to keep everything on the up-and-up.

"Wow! So, I take it he is the real deal?"

"Absolutely, without a doubt! He has a wonderful gift, but more than that, he is a wonderful man. I have been with him for a long time now, and he is more than a boss to me. . . . He is family. He is one of the sweetest, kindest, most caring men you will ever know. I was so worried about leaving him high and dry, but then he found you. Let's just say he has a good gut, so if he trusts you, well then, I trust you."

Patty, who was moved by the compassion and passion of her words, took a moment before speaking. "Well, thank you. I must say it would be hard not to do a good job with the resources and information you have given me."

"No problem. Once again, thanks so much for helping out. It makes an extremely difficult situation much less stressful." She hesitated a second before asking Patty a question. "Just out of curiosity, did this offer come about when he was doing a reading on you?"

"Why, no, it did not. As a matter of fact, he has not done a reading on me. He has only relayed messages from my sister. I think I may need to ask for a reading, though!"

"You definitely should. I assure you, it will blow you away!"

"Well, now I am excited. Thanks again for all your help. Don't worry about us. We will muddle through, I'm sure. Take care of your mom and yourself."

"Will do. Thanks again, and call or text if you have questions."

Patty hung up the phone and sipped her tea in silence, thinking about all that had happened in the past two days. It sure was a whirlwind, with so many unanswered questions and a great deal of uncertainty, but there were two things she was certain of—Peter was legitimate, and Sharon was using him to communicate with them. She tilted her head upward and whispered to the sky, "What, Sharon? What are you trying to tell us?"

Twenty-Two

K ayaking would be out of the question since the sun would go down before he arrived home, the warm temperatures of the day plummeting, ushering in a cold autumn night. Since he would not be venturing out in his kayak, he decided to pick up some food and drop by his mom's house to have dinner with her. Peter knew the missed kayaking opportunity was not the only reason he wanted to spend time with his mom. This business with Sharon and her family had more than a minor impact on him. He was reminded of the amazing bond between a mother and child. It also reminded him how precious life is and how everything can change in the blink of an eye; someone we love may be taken from us forever. And God knows he loved his mother.

The excitement was apparent in her voice when Peter phoned to tell her he was in the area and would like to have dinner with her. He told her he would pick up pizza and wings, his mom's guilty pleasure, and be there in time to eat dinner while watching *Jeopardy*.

"Oh, honey, that would be wonderful! Are you sure it's not a problem?"

"Not a problem at all! I've been so busy the past couple of weeks that I haven't been able to see you, but I have an open Saturday night and would love to hang out with you."

"Okay, that is great! I'll leave the light on for you."

Peter couldn't help but smile, hearing his mom say her favorite expression. Peter knew that those seven words were packed with so much emotion; I love you, stay safe, and this is always your home. He was surprised by how sentimental he was feeling. It had been an emotional few days, and he was thankful to be so close to his mom, as she was always his safe haven. His relationship with his dad was okay at best, but his dad was more distant than his mom and worked so much; he never developed the same closeness with him. His dad was also a little freaked out by Peter's apparent gift, which put an extra strain on their relationship. He was obviously embarrassed by what his son did for a living, although he never said as much. Peter and his mom both knew he would have been thrilled if Peter had chosen to do anything else. Anything.

Peter and his dad never talked about it, and they never would. John Dorjen passed away from a massive heart attack years ago. Without warning, he was gone, gone forever. That memory was weighing heavy on his mind when he was driving to his mom's. He dreaded the day she would leave this world and only hoped that would not be soon. But given her advanced years, he knew it probably wouldn't be too much longer. He could only hope that maybe she would find a way to communicate with him like Sharon had.

The evening turned out to be just what Peter needed. Judging by the colors he could see surrounding his mom—coupled with the smile on her face and laughter in her voice—it was exactly what she needed too. They ate and watched her favorite show, *Jeopardy*, which she was amazing at. When the show was over, Peter said, "Mom, you really ought to go on that show!"

"I'm just waiting for them to have a senior tournament. I mean, they have kids' week, college week, celebrity week . . . every week imaginable except for senior week."

"Maybe because that wouldn't be a trivia game but more like a memory test," Peter quipped while pouring them each a cup of coffee.

While enjoying their coffees, Peter filled her in on the events of the past few weeks. "I'm so sorry to hear about Marlee's mom. Send her my best, please."

She was intrigued and fascinated that he had a "spirit visitor" and was hanging onto his every word as he told her the story. He even shared that he could not read Patty at all. Her response baffled him. "Well, you never could see colors around yourself, could you?"

"Nope, still can't, Mom. Still can't, but always have seen things around everyone else."

"Hmmmm . . . that is interesting now, isn't it?" Peter's mom smiled.

"It seems to me that you find it more amusing than interesting."

"Well, for all your wonderful abilities, there are some things you are blind to."

"Oh, really? Okay, so why don't you enlighten me?"

"I know I don't share your psychic gifts, but it seems to me you may have found your soul mate."

Twenty-Three

The almost full parking lot was the first indication that Bailey's was a hopping place. "Do you want to try somewhere else?" John asked Katie when he saw the line waiting to get in.

"Nah. It's a beautiful night out, and I don't mind waiting," Katie replied while putting on her sweatshirt.

"See if you can find a bench while I give them our name."

Katie was able to procure a bench in front of the restaurant. It was under an old maple tree and was located slightly away from the crowd. Katie was thankful because, even twelve years after her mom's disappearance, she could feel the accusatory stares some of the guests gave her father. Many of the patrons did not know them from Adam, did not recognize them at all. There were people oblivious to their past, people who had never heard their story. However, there were still some that not only knew the story but were sure that John got away with murder.

She hedged the subject while waiting for a table and posed a question that was on her mind. "Why keep the house in Harperstown? Why not sell it and get a place closer to the city?"

"Because it's our home. It's your home."

"I know, but home is not a building. Home is people, and you and Patty will always be my home. Thanks for providing me with such a wonderful place to grow up, but news flash . . . I'm grown up!"

"You certainly are, and your mom would be so proud of you. I know I am."

"I know you are, and now I know mom is as well."

The look on her face as she spoke those words threatened

to bring a tear to John's eye, but thankfully he was saved by the phone's vibration, alerting them that their table was ready.

John and Katie enjoyed their night out as the conversation took on a less serious tone. They talked about school, the Fall Fest, and even made some holiday plans. Katie suggested that they spend Christmas in the city.

"I can come there and see you. Patty can come too. I have always wanted to spend Christmas in New York City. We could go see the Rockettes Christmas show!" Katie spoke with such enthusiasm that John had to stifle his laughter.

"Sounds like you have this all figured out. Let me get through the rest of this weekend, and I will look into Christmas in the city."

"That's a deal." Katie reached her hand out to shake on it.

Katie enjoyed a wonderful dinner and a delicious dessert with her father. She felt so relaxed and happy that she thought talking to Peter put an end to the weirdness of the last couple of weeks. That thought was put to an abrupt end as she was making her way to the restroom. As she walked past the bar, fear overtook her. She found it hard to breathe, hard to think, and hard to keep walking. Somehow, she managed to put one foot in front of the other and made her way to the restroom. With a few splashes of cold water on her face, she regained her composure enough to make her way back to the table, looking pale and a little out of sorts.

"Are you okay?" John asked, concerned.

"I'm fine. I'm just stuffed. I am not accustomed to eating like this." Katie forced herself to smile so her dad wouldn't worry.

Twenty-Four

For the second night in a row, he lay perfectly still on his bed. With the planning complete, all he had to do was go over the details. Eyes closed, he meticulously went over every detail. He watched the events unfold like a movie—a movie where he was writer, director, star, and dare he say . . . hero. The anticipation resulted in tiny beads of sweat building up on his forehead. He never sweated when he was hot or angry or worried, but he sweated like a teenage boy in gym class when he was excited, and man was he excited tonight! The act of visualizing always thrilled him, as did the moments right before he went into action. Tonight, though, the excitement was taken to another level, a level he had never felt before, at least not to this degree. He was aware that do-overs don't happen often in life, and they definitely don't happen in death, but this was as close to a do-over as one could hope for, which is why he could feel his adrenaline flowing, why he was certain it was fate.

This second chance to get it right provided more opportunities than he could have dreamed of. Fate was like that, though. When something is destined to happen, the pieces simply fall into place without much effort at all. This was the case over the last two weeks. Even actions that feel like a mistake—causing a bit of panic and a good deal of anxiety—worked out and fit into fate's plan as if they were part of the story. Just like it had with Brittany. . . . Was that her name? No, not Brittany . . . Barb? No . . . Beth! It was definitely Beth! Beads of sweat began rolling down the side of his face as he remembered her. His mind quickly shifted from planning the next event to replaying the last one.

Beth was a perfect example of improvisation and seizing an opportunity. It was dusk when he first saw her. She was alone, upset and alone. Walking, well, storming, down the almost deserted road. If it weren't for his car and her, it would have been entirely deserted. As the car drew closer to her, he eased his foot off the accelerator and onto the brake. Using the button on his driver's side door, he lowered the passenger side window. She raised her head to look at him. Her tearstained face and distraught expression could not hide her beauty. In fact, it just made her appear more fragile. Moving quickly, he grabbed the coat that was on the seat and ran to her. "Are you okay?" he asked, raising the chloroform-soaked cloth to her face. She was a petite girl, couldn't weigh over ninety pounds, which made placing her into the car an easy task. As the car pulled away, the only thing left behind was a book bag that fell off her shoulder as she succumbed to the chloroform. In what he thought was a moment of genius, with a gloved hand, he placed a copy of a broken heart picture in her book bag. When he was done with her, with assistance from the lake, he would make sure her body would never be found.

Sunday

—— ◆ ——

OCTOBER 24, 2017

Twenty-Five

Peter woke early after restless bouts of fitful sleep. The bombardment of his own thoughts, combined with the plethora of images shown by Sharon, made his head a busy place. While groggily taking small sips of his hot coffee, a new image appeared. He became accustomed to the puzzle with the missing pieces, the hourglass, the numbers, the initials, the white cloth, and, of course, the painted heart with a jagged line cutting through the middle. This image was new and quite different. It was the title of a newspaper with the date clearly visible.

It was a newspaper he had never heard of before, so he would need to use the internet to see if he could locate it. He quickly discovered that he was justified in complaining about the ease with which one can access information on the computer. No wonder so many people were attempting to capitalize on fake psychic abilities. In no time at all, he found the newspaper and read an article about the misconception we have of serial killers. It stated that a large percentage of serial killers lead very normal lives; they appear to be everyday, average people who hold jobs and often have wives and children who are completely unaware of their loved one's dark, secret life. The article went on to say that it's not the way they are frequently portrayed in movies and TV. Hollywood's version of serial killers differs greatly from reality's version. Most serial killers are not crazy loners. Many manage to commit these horrific acts for years and years without getting caught. When they are apprehended, they often confess, which is how the authors of this article came to their conclusion. *Sharon, what are you trying to tell me? Why did you direct me to this rather disturbing article?*

Peter was completely baffled. He knew it had something to do with her, but he could not figure out what the connection might be. *Are you trying to tell me that your murderer was a serial killer?* His head was spinning as his thoughts swirled around. *Could it be John? The normal dad, the perfect husband with a good job by day, serial killer by night?* That seemed like an obvious explanation; however, it made little sense to him, and as soon as the thought formed in his mind, he heard a chuckle that he assumed was from Sharon. He just couldn't fathom John having had anything to do with Sharon's disappearance. He had the strongest feeling that she was trying to tell him who was responsible for her death. That feeling was cemented when he saw a puzzle piece move into place. *I'm trying, Sharon . . . I'm trying!*

A good place to start would be to talk to Patty to get some more details about what happened the day Sharon went missing. For their first psychic reading event, they were going to ride together, which would give Peter ample opportunity to ask her questions. Since Marlee had already filled Patty in on her to-dos at events, Peter was confident that Patty knew her responsibilities. This would allow for plenty of time on the ride to get details on the events surrounding Sharon's disappearance.

On the way to the event, Patty and Peter sat in Peter's Lincoln Navigator. Patty had to admit that she was enjoying herself more than a little. As the car made its way along the lake, they engaged in conversation that covered a wide range of subjects— the weather, kayaking, and discussing if Patty's favorite football team, the Browns, would win a single game this season. "Maybe, but not against my Steelers!" Peter said teasingly. "Guess who has tickets to the Steelers versus Browns game in December?"

"You don't! Ugh, I'm so jealous! I don't think I like you anymore," Patty teased back.

"Tell you what . . . if you save me during Marlee's absence, I will bring you to the game with me." Patty squealed, and Peter paused before continuing, "A huge Browns fan gave the tickets to me. They are amazing seats on the fifty-yard line."

"Browns fan, huh? Why the heck did he give them to you, a Steelers fan?" Patty made a face as if she had just sucked on a lemon.

"Nice face!" Peter could not hold back a chuckle. "His wife was at an event I was doing, and I did a reading on her. I saw a health issue with her husband and told her he needed to get it checked immediately. It was more serious than he thought. Apparently, I was right! She went home and told him what I said. Her husband told her some symptoms he was having but kept them to himself. Well, to make a long story short, he saw a doctor right away, which apparently was a good thing. They discovered a fast-growing tumor, which they were able to remove surgically. He is completing treatments now! I ran into him and his wife at the grocery store, and I just happened to be wearing my Steelers shirt. Well, as I said earlier, he is a huge Browns fan." Peter mimicked the lemon face Patty made before continuing, "Not only a fan but a season ticket holder. He was so grateful for the alert I gave his wife, he insisted on giving me his two seats for the Steelers game, which he would not be able to attend anyway."

"Wow! That is an awesome story! I will do my best to keep things running smoothly in Marlee's absence, and not just for the ticket." Patty smiled. "I do believe I have some big shoes to fill."

Peter was enjoying the conversation greatly but knew he needed to find out more about Sharon's disappearance. While trying to figure out how to switch the subject, he noticed he was running low on gas and veered off the next exit to hit a gas station. While he pumped gas, Patty went into the store to get them each something to drink. Peter found himself watching her walk into the store. He was surprised that he still could not get a read on her but realized it no longer bothered him or caused him anxiety. In fact, he was quite enjoying her company.

Twenty-Six

Ethan woke up earlier than usual, which did not surprise him, but it left him feeling quite tired. *Ugh . . . and I have a seven-hour drive to look forward to,* he thought. He stayed in bed for a bit longer, tossing and turning, in a futile attempt to get some much-needed sleep. It did not take long before he succumbed to the fact that sleep was not going to happen and settled for a hot shower before heading downstairs.

The aroma of freshly brewed coffee filled the air as he approached the kitchen. He was surprised to see Edward already up and seated at the table. The sight of him sent anxiety surging through his body.

He had grown accustomed to Edward making him feel anxious . . . uncomfortable . . . nervous, and he wasn't sure why. After all, Edward seemed like a great guy. He checked all the boxes. He was kind, caring, reliable, and a good provider, but to Ethan, it felt like he was playing a role and purposefully trying to check all the boxes. He began to feel somewhat differently about Edward while staying with him, which is why he was taken aback by the return of discomfort and anxiety.

"Good morning!" Edward greeted him with a little too much energy. "Coffee is ready," he said, pointing toward the counter that held the coffeepot. "You know where the mugs are."

"Thanks, I am in dire need of a cup this morning."

"I am sure you are. What do you have left to do?" Edward asked.

"Just loading the car up, which could be as challenging as solving a Rubik's Cube." Ethan chuckled.

The two men sipped their coffees in silence. Edward read

the newspaper while Ethan scrolled through his phone. Ethan broke the lengthy silence when he said, "Thanks for everything you've done for me, letting me go through your home and take my mom's old belongings, allowing me to crash here, and of course, the car!"

"No problem. I know your mom would want you to have all of it."

"Yeah, I know. But thanks for holding onto everything for so long. I really appreciate it."

"I know you do, but don't go getting all sappy on me. You've got a long drive ahead of you, so how about I make us some bacon and eggs, and you can set the table and make some toast?"

"Sounds like a plan," Ethan replied.

The two men sat down at the kitchen table surrounded by smells of bacon, coffee, and toast. The kitchen seemed to transform into a greasy diner. Few words were exchanged as they both wolfed down the contents of their plates as if they had not eaten in years.

It was while he was doing dishes that he caught a glimpse of the old typewriter in the other room. It had a paper hanging out of it as though someone had just finished typing. Drying his hands off on the dish towel, he headed toward the old machine. He pulled the paper out, gently releasing it from the old Remington, and began reading. The words on the paper seemed to swirl in his head. He was desperately trying to process what he was reading, trying to make sense of it. He found himself in a state of utter confusion. "Whaa . . . whaaaa . . . whaattt is this?" The words struggled to escape his mouth. Hearing footsteps behind him, he turned his head, and his world went black.

Twenty-Seven

A s soon as the hot water rolled over her body, Katie could feel the release of emotions that had welled inside her over the past two days. She stood for minutes, just letting the water trickle down her back. Peter's unexpected arrival, combined with her 3:24 wake-up call for over two weeks now, left her feeling a contradictory combination of tired and tense. She hoped that sleeping in her dad's house would result in a dreamless sleep, but that was not the case. She awoke at exactly 3:24 in an extremely frightened and panicked state. Her entire body filled with tension, she decided to skip her morning run, opting instead for a shower to ease her neck pain, pancakes, black coffee, and a relaxing morning.

As much as she enjoyed being home, she was looking forward to getting back to campus and the distraction the festival would provide. So much had happened over the past couple of days, and she felt the need to process it in small doses. The bombardment of information had her struggling to maintain her sanity. *Sanity? What sanity? I'm having reoccurring nightmares, listening to a psychic, and I believe my mom's talking to us from the grave. I think it's safe to say I'm way past having a grip on my sanity.*

After an unusually long shower, Katie emerged from the bathroom feeling significantly better. She quickly gathered her items and headed downstairs. For a moment, she felt as if she was ten years old, bounding down the stairs to see her mom. It still amazed her how life can change in the blink of an eye. The world you know and count on simply crumbles to the ground, leaving rubble and shattered pieces where love and security once stood. As she took the last step, she had the strangest feeling that her mom was right behind her. Of course, a quick glance over her shoulder brought her back to reality.

John, who was in the kitchen, heard Katie moving around directly above him and had her pancakes ready before she came down the stairs. He was reminded of when she was younger and still lived here. Nostalgia seemed to be the theme of the weekend, thanks in large part to Peter. He still didn't know what to think of the whole thing. Although, even he had to admit, this Peter fella did more than just awaken memories. He gave John a gift that freed him more than he could have hoped. Ever since Sharon's disappearance, John had a hard time truly embracing or fully enjoying any of Katie's events. Whether it was a school concert or graduation, he always felt a sadness accompanied by a tinge of guilt. He was able to be there to witness their daughter's events, achievements, and even disappointments. Sharon was not . . . or was she? This Peter guy's readings gave him more than a little hope that she was watching them—and she was with them always. This not only comforted him but freed him in some way.

With all the talk about Sharon's disappearance, John's mind could not focus on much else. He kept reliving the past in his head. As he was sipping on a warm coke and straightening up the kitchen, which was presently doing double duty as a kitchen and dining room, his mind drifted back to the time when he agreed to let Katie stay in town with Patty. He wanted nothing more than to keep her life as stable as possible. Patty and John agreed that was best. Besides, they both knew stability was what Sharon would have wanted. A downfall of this decision was that it allowed for John to pretend that life really hadn't changed. At least during the week when he was working, he could simply pretend that Katie was at home with Sharon. Evening after evening with no contact with Sharon proved to be a slap in the face from reality. So, he worked thirteen-to-fifteen-hour days,

Monday through Thursday, but not Friday. On Fridays, he was the first one out of the office. He always tried to beat Katie home. She would find him sitting in the oversized Adirondack chair on the front porch or in the kitchen baking her favorite snack of chocolate chip cookies.

Katie popped her head into the kitchen. "Hey, Dad! How's it going?"

"Good morning, sweetheart. It's going well." He was relieved to see her looking a little better than the night before. "Are you heading out?"

"Yepper, I want to help Ally with the festival. I am going to have to get on the road in a few minutes," Katie said, looking at the time on her phone.

"Well, please take care of yourself and don't work too hard. You look a bit tired . . . and, well . . . you are getting older," her dad said with a smile. The smile hid the concern he was feeling.

A mere fifteen minutes later, Katie was on her way out the door. As she made her way to the car, John yelled, "Don't forget, I want a safe arrival text!"

"You got it!" Katie shouted back.

John watched as the car pulled away. Unbeknownst to him, he was not the only one watching Katie drive away.

Twenty-Eight

With a tank full of gas and bottles of water in hand, Peter and Patty were on the road again. They continued the small talk for a bit, but before long, the conversation inevitably made its way to Sharon. "As odd as it seems, I really know very little about Sharon's disappearance. I think it might be helpful if I did. Would you mind filling me in?" Peter asked.

"I don't know much either. Therein lies the problem. It's as if Sharon was here one moment and then . . . not here . . . gone . . . poof, like a bad magic trick."

For the remainder of the hour-long ride, Patty filled Peter in on the days surrounding Sharon's disappearance. "The first days—really weeks—were a blur, like a tornado ripped through my life. I went through the motions, but when I try to remember, it is all a blur. Search parties, police officers asking endless questions, microphones being thrust in my face, flashes going off every time I would leave the house, which was usually to go answer more of the never-ending questions, questions that got us nowhere . . . questions without answers. I remember feeling so . . . mmmm . . . so confused. It was as if they put me in a scene of a movie, but someone forgot to give me the script. In the end, there were no answers. Sharon, wife, mother, sister, appeared to have simply vanished into thin air. For years, I imagined her walking through the door with some crazy amnesia story. You know, like in the movie *Overboard*. As the years rolled on, I imagined it less and less. After seven years, they declared her legally dead. No ceremony, no funeral, no body, and no answers, not even a solid suspect!"

"I can't even imagine. That had to be a nightmare."

"The first few days, all my attention was on Katie. With John as a prime suspect, I . . . I had to attend to Katie. As confused as I felt, I knew there was no way John had anything to do with any of this. Oh, my God, if he did . . . Katie would have lost both parents in the blink of an eye. After about a week, John was cleared. I should say cleared by the police . . . as for the townspeople, well, that was a different story."

She paused to gain her composure, surprised by how difficult it was to talk about even after all this time. "One by one, the short list of suspects, including John, a teenage boy named Ethan, and a plumber who was working in the neighborhood, oh, yeah, and me . . . my name was on the list . . . it did not take too long before we were all cleared because of solid alibis, lack of motive, and lack of evidence."

Peter found himself at a loss for words. *Say something . . . say something, anything.* He remained silent and gave an empathetic nod. It pained him to hear her story, but he was hanging on to every word. Normally, when speaking with someone, he sees colors encircling them, giving him insight into what they're feeling, beyond the words they're saying. With Patty, he had no inkling as to what she was feeling. He paused a moment before he said, "And?"

"And, just like all the others, nothing came of it. That is, as far as the police were concerned. In town, you would hear many theories, all stated as facts, all created by couch detectives."

This brought a chuckle out of Peter. "May I render a guess that one of them was that John must have hired someone to do it?"

"Yep . . . and he did so because he and I were having an affair." Just the thought made her blood boil. "Like I would have ever done that to my sister. Not to mention Katie!"

"People like to hear themselves talk. What other theories were the talk of the town?"

"That Ethan boy . . . many people felt he was responsible. Some people thought maybe he did it for John. He was fairly new to town, here less than a year when his mom took her own life. It was sad. So incredibly sad. It happened not long before Sharon disappeared. Ethan was . . . well . . . a bit . . . awkward . . . quiet . . . one might say *strange*, which made it easy for people to talk about him. Suicidal mom, homicidal son."

"Wow! That is harsh. Doesn't sound like you agreed with that assessment?"

"No, I didn't. I mean, I don't know the details of what happened to his mom. I only know she passed away from an overdose, Ambien, I believe. Sharon and Ethan formed a bond around that time. He was in an after-school art program that Sharon ran. She said he had quite a gift. After his mom passed, Sharon went out of her way to make sure he would keep attending her sessions. Sharon had a way with people, and Ethan was no exception. She convinced him to let her display some of his work, and I must say he was very talented. That's neither here nor there. He has long been off the police radar. He was home with his stepdad all night when Sharon went missing. I never thought he did it. Sharon liked him, and he liked her, not in a freaky way but as a teacher or mentor. Kid had it rough and didn't have any friends around here. He always seemed a bit out of place, but being an awkward, sad teenager doesn't make you a psychopathic killer, although, in this town, it could."

"What ever came of this Ethan boy?"

"As I said, he had recently moved here with his mom and her new husband when she tragically died. Ethan did not know anyone in town—he hardly knew his stepfather. He stayed around for a little while, but a few months after Sharon's disappearance, he went to Virginia to live with his mom's brother and his family. Haven't seen hide nor hair of him since. I think about him sometimes, though; I hope things got better for him."

Peter could not help but admire her compassion and empathy. *She might just do alright today.* "Is his stepdad still around?"

"Yep, he is. Still lives in the same lake house. A nice place called The Crow's Nest. Clever name being his last name is Crow."

Peter hesitated a moment before deciding to hold off on telling Patty about an image that was bombarding his brain—the initials EC. *Ethan . . . Ethan Crow.*

Twenty-Nine

Patty was surprisingly relaxed as she spoke to the full room. It was as if she had been Peter's assistant forever. The words poured effortlessly from her mouth. She and Peter seemed in sync, like choreographed dancing partners. She enjoyed the entire experience of assisting Peter—and simply being with him—even more than she thought she would.

The event was a tremendous success, and Peter left his audience longing for more. Patty enjoyed seeing him like this. He seemed so at ease, as if he was at home in his natural element, different from how he seemed when talking to them about Sharon. Patty said as much to him on the trip home.

"That obvious, is it?" Peter replied with a shake of his head.

"Not in a bad way . . . it's just . . . well . . . you seemed so confident . . . at ease . . . in complete control."

"Well, I've been doing this sort of thing my whole life. It is a part of who I am, but this whole deal with your sister, Sharon, now that's new to me and, to be quite honest, it's got me a bit rattled."

"Really? This is that different?" Patty inquired.

"Oh, yes, it is. Seeing colors and images around people, getting a general gut feeling or hunch is just how I see people. It's how I've always seen people. Well, most people, anyway." Peter decided not to elaborate on the fact that he saw nothing when he looked at her. No colors, no images, nothing. "Over the years, I've developed—one might even say I've fine-tuned—my skills into a kind of art form. Let's just say nothing like what's happening now, with Sharon, has ever happened to me before."

"Really? That would be my sister, always finding new ways to communicate," Patty said with a chuckle.

"I just wish I knew I was handling it correctly. I feel so . . . so . . . out of control. Like I'm winging it and am always a step or two behind, like I am missing something, missing something big. To top it off, I feel bad that I have crashed into you and your family's life, turning it upside down. I just really felt like I didn't have a choice, but I am so sorry I brought this all back to you . . . Sharon's disappearance and all the painful memories. I'm deeply sorry," Peter said tenderly.

"Oh, don't be sorry. I believe we needed this, all of us, but especially Katie. We needed to remember the past . . . to talk about it . . . about Sharon."

"I'm glad you feel that way, but . . ." His voice faded.

"But . . . but what?" Patty responded.

"Well, just between you and me, I don't think that is all I'm supposed to do."

"Go on."

"I feel like I'm not only supposed to help solve Sharon's disappearance, but . . . I don't want to scare you . . ."

"What? Peter . . . what?" Patty said in an anguished tone.

"Well, I have this feeling . . . a very strong feeling that Katie is in danger."

"Oh, my God! Why? How? When?"

"I don't know those answers. As I told you, I am new to this. I wish I knew the answers to your questions. I wish I knew what Sharon is trying to communicate to me, but I don't. I'm sorry, but I don't."

"Why do you feel this way? Please, Peter! Please, don't keep anything from me. Maybe I can help. I know Sharon better than anybody. So, I need to know everything. Everything . . ." The tone of Patty's command reminded him of Sharon.

"Okay . . . okay. I can fill you in over an early dinner, but you better bring a notebook and pen. I guess you should know everything." Patty, who already had a notebook and pen in her hand, simply nodded. "Alright, it's settled, but now I need you to look up the Sparkling Falls Diner," Peter said.

"Okay, is that near here?"

"Couldn't tell you. That's why I need you to look it up."

Looking at her phone, Patty said, "Okay, but it's not on the way home. In fact, it is ten minutes out of the way. Is the food that good?"

"Couldn't tell you that either, but judging by the urgent nature of the images flashing in my mind and knowing what I know about your sister, we are going to have to find out."

Without another word, Patty set her Google Maps and started giving Peter directions. "Wow! I'd think you wouldn't need me or Google Maps. Why, with your super psychic abilities, you should know exactly where you're going." Patty chuckled.

"Well . . . I see you walking home if you keep it up," Peter teased back.

Thirty

H e watched from behind the steering wheel of the BMW. He had a bird's-eye view of the Parish home and was relieved to see Katie, overnight bag in hand, get into her car and drive away. *Headed back to her apartment*, he presumed. In fact, his plan depended on it.

Following her car was unnecessary since he had already scouted out her apartment and made himself familiar with the surrounding area. All part of his meticulous planning and preparation, he stayed a few cars behind her, close enough to keep an eye on her but far enough not to attract attention.

He watched her enter the apartment from the driver's seat of the Beemer. He noted she used her key to unlock the door, leading him to conclude she was alone. *Hmmm, could this be another unexpected opportunity? Another of fate's wonderful surprises, perhaps? Her being alone in the apartment, that would make it so easy to have a little fun before getting her out of there and back to the house.* As much as the thought of enjoying a little afternoon delight with her was tempting, he knew that would be reckless. There would be plenty of time once they were out of here and back at his secluded house. After wrestling with his own demons for a while, the sound of his voice broke the silence in the car. "No time like the present." Patting his coat pocket to reassure himself that he still had the sealed baggie containing a chloroform-soaked cloth, he prepared to exit the car and make his presence known. Just as he opened the door, he saw Katie emerge from her apartment. She headed down the steps, through the yard, and around the corner, and in a matter of seconds, she was out of sight.

Because he was in the process of getting out of the car, he caught up to her quickly. As soon as she turned off the street and made her way through the quad, the crowd seemed to appear out of nowhere. As much as he was not a fan of crowds and usually avoided them whenever he could, this time, the crowd helped make it easier for him to be inconspicuous. With his baseball cap, sunglasses, and hoodie on, he most certainly did not stand out. In fact, he blended in perfectly. As soon as he realized she would be working in the tent serving drinks, he took a seat under a nearby tree that gave him a perfect view of her. Watching her move about pouring drinks and laughing added to his anticipation of what awaited him. Despite the cooler fall temperatures, beads of sweat were forming on his brow.

Thirty-One

Katie expected Ally to be surprised that she returned for the last day of the festival, but the look on her face, not to mention her elated screech, far surpassed Katie's expectations. Without a doubt, Katie was sure she made the right decision about returning home. It sure didn't take Ally any time at all to put Katie to work with—she should have guessed it—Shane. They were working at one of the makeshift bar tents. Katie was taking orders, and Shane was pouring drinks. Not surprisingly, beer was the drink of choice, with wine a distant second.

There was a line as far as Katie could see, which kept her and Shane hopping. It also kept her from fixating on recent events, which was a good thing, and it showed in the relaxed smile on her face as she greeted customers and joked with Shane. It was surprising her how much she was enjoying herself. The work was a welcome distraction, not to mention the festive, celebratory feeling that was contagious. Katie couldn't help but feel happy and lighthearted. All the sadness and anxiety seemed to vanish, except for one intense but short-lived panic attack. It came on while she was waiting on a customer. The customer dropped her money, and when she bent over to retrieve it, Katie was left with an unobstructed view of a man sitting under a nearby tree. Although she did not recognize the man, as soon as she caught sight of him, her body was paralyzed with the intense feeling of panic.

Shane saw the look on Katie's face and immediately came to her assistance. He grabbed her by the arm and guided her into a chair in the corner near where she was standing. Without missing a beat, he took a few orders. As he turned to pour the drinks, he approached Katie. The color returned to her face. "You okay?"

"I'm fine," she answered, standing up.

"You sure?"

"I am good, but I could use some water."

"Here you go," he said, handing her a bottle of water. "And since you won't be going anywhere for a while, eat this." He smiled while handing her Snickers.

The hours were flying by. She would work until seven, then run back to the apartment to shower and change before heading over to the main quad, where she would meet up with Ally to enjoy the last event of the festival, a concert by an extremely popular up-and-coming local band. With all the planning and major work done, Ally and Katie were going to take this concert in purely as spectators. It was hard to imagine Ally having any energy left, but Katie knew Ally and was sure that she would appear as though she had just woken up.

Thirty-Two

————— •◆• —————

The GPS informed them they had arrived at their destination. Peter held the door open as Patty entered the small diner and found it quite crowded, which Peter and Patty took as a good sign. As soon as they were seated at a cozy corner table that appeared to be the last open seat, a slightly overweight, pleasant woman took their drink order.

"Can I interest you in an appetizer? Half price on our fried pickles today, and they are delicious!"

"Would you like to try some?" he asked Patty.

"Sure, let's give them a try."

"I will put the order in and be right back with your drinks," the waitress said while walking away.

They quietly shared the tasty fried pickle appetizer, and while enjoying a delicious burger, Peter explained the details of his experiences over the past two weeks. Spending the day with her had a positive effect on him. He was no longer troubled by the fact that Patty was an unreadable mystery to him. He was actually enjoying the normalcy it brought with it. At first, he wondered if it was a bad thing that he could not get a read on her and did not see any colors surrounding her, but his instincts told him it wasn't bad, just different. Looking at the present state of his life, different was the new normal.

In between bites, he told her about his bouts of sickness and nausea while driving to the reading the day before and again at John's house. He filled her in on the shouts from Sharon: "*Couldn't save myself . . . must save her!*" Those words seemed to freak Patty out. Peter, seeing the look on Patty's face, paused. "I'm sorry."

"Don't be . . . don't be sorry. I want to know everything. I want to help you. No, I want to help Sharon and Katie."

Peter continued talking. He told her how it all started. Then he filled her in on the events leading up to the birthday luncheon. He told her about the newspaper article about serial killers, as well as the images he kept seeing—the emptying hourglass, the puzzle with missing pieces, the numbers three, two, and four, a white hanky, the broken heart painting, and the initials EC.

Patty, who was diligently writing everything down, looked up and said, "Okay . . . let's take these one at a time. The numbers three, two, and four seem to represent the time Katie wakes up from a nightmare every night."

"True. That's what I thought, but that leads me to wonder why. Why is she having the same nightmare, at the same time every night?"

"Maybe that is the time Sharon went missing," Patty responded.

"Hmmm. You are good at this. Alright, let's go with that. Now the way I see it, the puzzle is Sharon's way of telling me . . . us . . . that we are missing clues, and the hourglass says we are running out of time, which, for the record, I find extremely stressful!"

"I am with you on that! So, let's move on."

"As for the white hanky, I don't have a clue. It's just a plain white hanky. Does that mean anything to you?"

"Not a thing."

"Now the heart. The heart is the most frequent and by far the clearest."

"What exactly does the heart look like?" Patty asked.

Before Peter could respond to Patty's question, the waitress was at their table with a dessert tray. She said in her enthusiastic voice, "Now for the crème de la crème. I hope you saved some room for our world-famous cheesecake."

"Ummm . . . I am quite full, but that looks good! Hey, Patty, would you like to split one?"

"I think I could help you out with one. . . . The cherry cheesecake sure looks good."

"You heard the lady, a cherry cheesecake to share, please."

"You got it, and I'm so confident you will love it, I bet you'll order one to go before you leave." She flashed a toothy grin and sauntered toward the kitchen.

Thirty-Three

Time continued to fly, and before Katie and Shane knew it, it was 7:00 p.m., and their replacements were there, not only ready but eager to take over. Katie gladly stepped aside and grabbed her phone as they vacated the tent to make room for the next shift.

"You heading over to the concert?" Shane asked as they walked out.

"Yes, but I have to head back to my apartment to change and clean up a bit first."

"Me too!" Shane laughed. "I think I got as much beer on me as I did in the cups! How about I walk . . ." Shane's sentence was interrupted by a familiar voice.

"Katie, Katie, wait up!" Ally cried out while running in their direction.

"What are you doing over here?" Katie shouted back.

Ally held her hand up, catching her breath as she approached Katie and Shane. "I . . . I ran over here, hoping to catch you. . . . I need a favor from you."

"Okay. But you could have called." Katie chuckled while holding her phone up.

"No, I couldn't." Ally smiled, holding her phone up as well. "It's dead! I was hoping you could charge it for me?"

"Not a problem. I was heading home to clean up a bit. I will place it on the quick charger and bring it back."

"Oh . . . you are a lifesaver!"

"Here, take my phone. God knows you can't survive without a phone!" Katie held her phone out to Ally.

"Are you sure?"

"Absolutely, the world is not ready for phoneless Ally," Katie teased.

The two women exchanged phones and headed in opposite directions. Shane insisted on walking Katie to her apartment, and since the only phone she had was Ally's, which was dead, she agreed. She wasn't sure if it was the weekend's events, exhaustion, or Shane, but whatever the reason, Katie found herself enjoying the evening stroll back to her apartment, so much so that she did not put up her usual wall. They made conversation easily as they walked side by side.

"I think I spilled so much booze on my shirt that it made me a little tipsy," Katie joked.

"Tipsy? You smell like a brewery. I'd say you might be downright hammered!" Shane teased in return.

"Funny thing is, I am looking forward to a cold one at the concert. It will be nice to relax."

"How about I come and pick you up on my way back, and we can walk over together? I'll even buy you that cold one when we get there."

Katie surprised herself with her response. "I'd like that. Can you give me a half an hour to get ready and to let Ally's phone charge?"

"That works," Shane responded, trying not to let his surprise or excitement show.

"Okay, well, this is our humble abode," she said, waving her arm toward the porch.

"Alright, I live right down the road, so I'll plan to come by in about thirty minutes. You have Ally's phone, right?"

"Yes, her dead phone."

"I will call her phone when I get close."

"Sounds good. That will be a good way to be sure I remember to bring it."

"Definitely . . . I can only imagine that a phoneless Ally is not a pretty sight!"

Shane stayed on the sidewalk until she made her way inside, and then he took off toward his apartment, which was not as close as he suggested. He did not want to be late, which wouldn't be a problem as he felt as if he was floating on air.

Thirty-Four

———— •◆• ————

"Mmmmm . . . mmmmm . . . mmmmm! This just might be the best cheesecake I've ever had!" Peter said in between bites.

Patty finished chewing and swallowing before she said, "I think I do need to order one to go!"

"You read my mind!" Peter chuckled.

"Speaking of reading minds . . . how about you give me a reading? Marlee said I'd love it, and you might even amaze me."

"Ummm . . . I'm afraid I can't do that."

"If it's the money, I'll pay you." *Maybe he is a con; maybe it's all about the money.*

"It's not about the money . . . believe me. I'd love to do a reading on you, but when I say I can't . . . I mean, I can't." Peter's face took on an expression of confusion. "I mean, I really can't do a reading on you. . . . It's not possible because when I look at you, I don't see anything. No colors, no symbols, nothing but you."

"Okay, now you are scaring me!"

"Scaring you?"

"Uh, yeah! I'm sure you have heard of the classic urban legend involving a lady's visit to a psychic?"

"Can't say that I have. I guess it's your turn to enlighten me."

"So, this lady schedules a reading with an extremely popular psychic who is in town. She arrives and takes a seat. The psychic promptly informs her he has an emergency and will be unable to read her today. He hands her an envelope, which he says contains instructions on how to get her money back plus a complimentary reading. He instructs her not to open it until she gets home. He claims he will know if she does, and that will void all deals and offers. The lady puts the note in her purse and heads home. Well, she never made it. She was hit by a car and died instantly. When given her purse, her husband opened the envelope and read the note, which simply said, *you have no future!* So, pardon me, but you are saying you can't read me. . . . Well, it's freaking me out a little."

Peter reassured her it was nothing like that. He let her know he has never seen colors or anything when he looks at her. "There was one other person, at a group event, that I could not read."

"That's it? One other person? Did they die right after the reading?"

Peter ignored the question, in part because he honestly didn't know the answer, although he wondered if his mom may be on to something with her theory of why he could not get a read on Patty. "Listen, I've never seen anything around myself. Not in a mirror or a picture . . . never! And I'm still kicking."

Peter was relieved to see their cheerful waitress return with a pot of coffee. As she topped off their cups, Peter placed the order for cheesecakes to go. Along with the cherry, he ordered two plain and two chocolate delights. When given the bill, he chuckled at the fact that he spent way more on cheesecakes than he did on everything else.

Patty reached into her purse to get money out for her part of the bill, but Peter resisted. "It's a work meeting, so it's on me."

"Alright, but I need at least one of those cheesecakes to go home with me." She chuckled in return.

"Consider it an apology gift for scaring the crap out of you!"

"Sounds fair," Patty agreed.

With full stomachs and bags filled with cheesecake, Patty and Peter headed to the exit of the restaurant. As Peter was putting on her coat for her, he spotted a missing persons poster that took his breath away. He looked Patty in the eyes and said,

"You know the vision of the heart I've been seeing? The one Sharon keeps showing me?"

"Yeah . . ."

He placed his hands on her shoulders and gently turned her around. "There it is!"

Patty was looking at an oversized poster of a missing girl. Mixed in with all the relevant information was a picture of a painting of a broken heart. It was red, with a jagged black break in it. It showed the backside which contained the word *BROKENHEARTED*. Patty's heart skipped a beat. After a moment, she said, "Peter . . . we have got to go . . . now!"

"Where?" Peter inquired with a puzzled expression.

"To John's house. I saw that heart there yesterday!"

Thirty-Five

*C*ould it be John? *It couldn't be . . . oh, my God . . . not John . . .* Peter's hands gripped the steering wheel so tightly that his knuckles were turning white. He looked over at Patty, who was sitting in the passenger seat. She was looking at the missing girl poster she took from the restaurant and the broken heart picture at the bottom. "It says anyone with any information about Beth or this heart picture, please call this number," Patty said, her voice breaking the silence in the car.

It was obvious to Peter how much seeing the heart affected Patty. He had not yet brought up the fact that the heart on the poster—the heart she saw at John's house, the heart they were racing toward now—was the exact heart Sharon had been showing him; in fact, that image flashed frantically in his head as he drove.

The only explanation that made any sense was that John was responsible for Sharon's disappearance. The only problem was that it really didn't make sense at all. And it just didn't feel right—not one bit. He knew he had to share what he was thinking with Patty. The mere thought caused him to grip the wheel even tighter.

Taking a deep breath, he said, "That heart on the poster . . . the one you said you saw at John's . . ."

"You mean the one I am sure I saw at John's?"

"Yes . . . that is not just similar to the broken heart I've been seeing. It *is* the broken heart picture I've been seeing. In fact, I am seeing it now!"

Patty let out an audible gasp before she said, "Oh, my God . . . Peter, what does this mean?"

"I wish I knew, but before I share my thoughts with you, you must promise to keep an open mind."

"Of course, Peter. What? What are you thinking?"

"Well, the broken heart being in John's possession . . . Sharon ensuring we went to the diner where we would most likely see that poster . . . and let's not forget the article about serial killers often living normal everyday lives with wives and children, appearing to be family men, fooling everyone for years and years, sometimes for a lifetime . . . it all seems to point to John."

Peter's words hit Patty hard. She immediately wanted to tell him he was wrong but knew she had to take a minute to absorb his words and process what he said. She was so engrossed in her thoughts that she was completely oblivious to the beautiful sunset occurring outside her window. After a few minutes, which seemed like hours to Peter, she said, "It can't be . . . not John. Everything in my gut says it can't be John."

"Mine too, but . . ."

"No buts! Aren't you the one who said, 'Always trust your gut'?"

"With that kind of memory, I don't know why you bother taking notes, and yes, I am the one who said that. I'm the one who always says that, as well as the one who lives by those words."

"Well, then live by them now. And step on it. We must get to John's house before it's too late." Too late for what, she didn't have a clue.

Patty burst through the front door and made her way to the dining room table. Her face turned ghost white as she lifted the paper from the table and stared at it. She trembled, and the picture slipped from her hands. It slowly floated downward before resting on the floor. Peter picked it up and turned it over. On the back, he saw the now familiar broken heart. He recognized it immediately as the exact same heart picture constantly flashing in his mind. Before Patty held the poster up for comparison, both he and Patty knew the pictures were a perfect match.

John entered from the backyard and noticed them standing at his kitchen table. "Hey, I didn't know you were coming over."

Patty looked at John. Unsure of what to say, she asked one simple question, "Where did this picture come from, John? Whose picture is it?"

"Why? What is so important about that picture?"

Patty held up the missing persons poster.

"Where did you get that?" John asked.

"I think the more important question is, where did you get this?" Peter asked, holding up the matching picture from John's table.

John's mind kicked into overdrive. His brain was spinning. He took the picture and said, "That was from Ethan. It was to Sharon . . . well, to me and Sharon. Shortly after she went missing, Ethan's stepdad brought it to me . . ."

As soon as John began to speak, Sharon's voice exploded in Peter's head. *"Not love! Not love! Save her! Please save her! Save her!"* It was so loud and clear, he was sure everyone in the room could hear it, but John went right on talking. "He said Ethan wanted us to have it, but he just could not bear coming over here. I remember because it made me feel sad. I guess I just threw it on top of one of Sharon's photo albums that ended up in the box, the box I had long since forgotten about."

The whole time John was talking, Sharon's voice continued to fill Peter's head. He saw the puzzle with the missing piece, the same puzzle he had been seeing, but this time, a piece was being put into place. The initials EC were flashing, as if on a neon sign. It was Peter that spoke next. "Oh, my God! EC. Ethan Crow!"

"But Ethan doesn't even live around here anymore," Patty said.

"He may not live here, but he is in town. I saw him getting gas the other day. He was driving his mom's old car. He looks the same as he did. A bit older, but the same."

Everything started to make sense in Peter's head. He felt an urgency, a need to hurry to save her. The her, he could only assume, was Katie. "I believe we need to talk with Ethan." When nobody moved, he said, "Now!"

Patty understood his urgency and was already using her phone to locate Ethan's stepdad's house. "I can't find a phone number, but I have an address. It's 324 Lakeview Drive."

"Did you say 324?" His head was now exploding with images—the hourglass, EC, the white hanky, and the numbers. "Let's go!" Peter headed for the door with Patty on his heels.

"Wait for me!" John yelled.

"No, we need you here in case we need you to do something. We will be right back," Peter said while running out the door. John stood puzzled as Patty slammed the door behind her.

Thirty-Six

Completely disregarding Patty and Peter's instructions to stay home, John was on his way to Katie's apartment. A mere twenty-five minutes after they left, he was halfway there. Using the Bluetooth feature in his car, he fervently and desperately placed call after call to Katie but to no avail. The calls were not going directly to voice mail, so he had to endure five to six rings on each call, which felt like an eternity. As soon as he heard, "Hi, this is Katie," he disconnected the call and tried again. He left messages the first few times, but after so many tries, he just hung up and tried again. He even tried Ally's phone, but his calls to her went directly to voice mail.

◆ ◆ ◆

As soon as Ally placed Katie's phone in the easy to access cell phone pocket, Tom, her right-hand man for the day, grabbed her and told her they needed her at the concert field. "Now!" The last crisis of the weekend, or so she hoped, took about a half an hour to resolve. She checked on the band and beer tent before handing the evening responsibilities to a very capable maintenance and event crew. Her work here was done! At last, it was time to relax and enjoy the show.

She promptly headed toward the area where she told Tom to have seats saved for them. She was hoping against the odds that Katie and Shane would come to the concert together. *My phone! I better call Katie so she doesn't forget it!* She reached into her purse and pulled out Katie's phone. She was surprised to see twenty-nine missed calls. Her surprise turned to panic when she realized that all the calls were from the same person, Katie's dad.

She immediately placed a call to her cell phone, which went straight to voice mail. She thought about calling Katie's dad but decided against that. Not knowing what else to do, she took off toward their apartment, pausing a moment to remind Tom to save the seats.

Thirty-Seven

Once again, he sat quietly in the driver's seat of the Beemer. He left his spot near the beer tent as soon as he overheard Katie say she needed to go home and change. He wanted—no, he needed—a good view so he could see her enter the apartment. Timing is everything. His breath caught for a minute when he saw her walking up the street. She was not alone! She was walking with someone. It was the guy she worked with all day. It would definitely complicate things if he went into the apartment with her. With bated breath, he gripped the steering wheel tightly as the couple stopped in front of Katie's apartment. He could feel the tension leave his body as he watched Katie enter the apartment alone and saw the fella making his way down the street. Crisis averted! The scare got his adrenaline flowing. He found himself untypically nervous and just wanted to get this done.

Thirty-Eight

Peter pressed his foot harder and harder down on the gas pedal. He saw Patty's lips moving, but the only words he could hear were Sharon's cries, "*Help her! Help her! Hurry . . . please . . . hurry!*" The words were exploding in his head. He knew Patty was on the phone with John but struggled to hear her over Sharon.

"She isn't answering? Well, keep calling her! Text her too! We are almost at Edward's house. Keep trying her!"

"I am and I will! Keep me posted on what you find at the Crow's Nest," he replied, leaving out the fact that he was calling her from his car and speeding toward Katie's apartment.

Peter's car tore into the driveway five minutes quicker than the GPS initially predicted. Patty hopped from the car before it came to a complete stop and was pounding on the door before Peter climbed the porch stairs. Patty's repeated pounding on the door was met with silence. In desperation, she turned the doorknob, but it was locked. She tried to see in the house but to no avail.

Peter, who had joined Patty on the porch, said, "Let's be sure Katie is alright. That's all we can do for now since nobody is home here." Peter was shouting in an effort to be louder than Sharon's voice, which continued to fill his head.

A mere fifteen feet from the door, Ethan, who had heard the pounding on the door, was trying to make his presence known, but the tape over his mouth muted his cries. His head was fuzzy and more than a little sore. Despite his confusion, he knew he had to get the attention of whoever was pounding at the door. He was acutely aware that his life depended on it—his life and Sharon's daughter's life. With all the energy he could muster, he shimmied his body to the armrest of the couch. Using his shoulder for leverage, he thrust his head backward. Pain shot through his head and neck as his head hit the lamp. The lamp wobbled but remained standing. With the last bit of energy he could muster, he thrust backward one more time. This time, the force of contact resulted in the lamp tumbling from the table and loudly smashing onto the floor.

Patty turned around and was heading toward the porch steps when she heard the loud shattering coming from inside. "What the hell was that?" she shouted at Peter as she abruptly changed direction and headed back toward the house. Peter, who also heard the loud crash, had Sharon screaming at him to get into the house. As Peter scanned the front of the house for an accessible window, Sharon's voice exploded in his head. *"Go now! Get in there! Now!"*

Without even thinking about it, Peter picked up a rock and used it to break the frosted glass on the side of the front door. As shattered pieces of glass fell all around them, he reached his hand in and unlocked the door. Peter and Patty entered the house together and could not believe their eyes. A young man who was tied and gagged lay on the floor near the couch. Patty rushed to him and immediately tore the tape from his mouth.

"Ethan? Oh, my God! Ethan?"

"You n-n-n-nnnneed to stop him!" Ethan struggled to get the words out.

"Stop who?"

"Edward! Stop him . . . stop him before he kills her!"

"Kills who?" Patty choked the words out.

"Mrs. Parish's daughter. . . . Please stop him!" Ethan said in a faint but urgent voice.

"Katie? Why would he kill Katie?

"Stop him! Please . . . please . . ."

Thirty-Nine

After a few minutes, Ethan had gathered his bearings enough to fill Peter and Patty in on the events of the morning. They listened intently as Ethan told his story. He stood up and wobbled unsteadily for a moment before heading toward the typewriter. The letter was sitting right next to the old machine. He grabbed the paper and handed it to Patty. "I found this in the typewriter this morning." Patty began reading out loud.

```
To the people of Harperstown,
This is my goodbye letter. Notice I didn't say suicide
letter, but since my work here is done, it is my
time to ride off into the sunset. Although this is
not how I had planned or envisioned it, life as
it often does has a plan of its own, which it laid
at my feet, and I simply rolled with it. I, Ethan
Parker, as my farewell gift to the town, will solve
the town's greatest mystery, the disappearance of
Sharon Parish. Sharon did not run away. Nor did
her husband have her killed. Sharon, like so many
others, was just too good for this world, so I took on
the task of freeing her . . . freeing them all
. . . Sharon, my mom, and countless others. Today, I
finish my task by reuniting Sharon's daughter with
her mother. Then I shall free myself!
```

Sincerely,

Ethan Parker

"I didn't write that, I swear, I didn't! Edward must have. The last thing I remember is finding and reading this and turning to see Edward behind me. . . . Next thing I knew, I was tied and gagged on the couch with someone pounding on the door . . ." Ethan trailed off.

Patty, in a state of utter confusion bordering on shock, was desperately trying to process the situation, which left her unable to take any action at all, but Peter was fully aware of the seriousness of the situation, and as long as Edward was out there, Katie was in danger! *EC—Edward Crow!* He wasn't sure how or why, but suddenly he knew exactly what to do.

Even though he hadn't talked to him in quite some time, the name popped into his head, accompanied by Sharon's shouts of *"Call him!"* He knew without a doubt that he needed to call Officer O'Malley. *Please be working tonight.* He had the police department number in his contacts since he worked with them quite a few times in the past. It was during those times that he forged a friendship with Patrick O'Malley. The last time he saw him, he could tell retirement was in his near future, but he knew he had to call him. He could only hope that he hadn't retired yet. With slightly shaking hands, he placed the call. On the third ring, Peter heard the familiar voice. "Granderson Falls Police Department. Officer O'Malley speaking."

"O'Malley, it's Peter, Peter Dorjen."

"Hey, Peter! How are you doing these days?"

"Not so good! I could really use your help."

"Sure thing, Peter. How can I help you?"

"I have good reason to believe a young lady is in danger . . .

serious danger. I need you to send a car over to check it out . . . please!"

Without skipping a beat, O'Malley asked for the address. When Peter gave it to him, he responded, "Got it. That is right near the festival. There are a few cars on their way there. I will put a call into one of them right now and tell them to stop by and check it out. What is her name?"

"Her name is Katie, Katie Parish. Thanks! Please hurry!"

"Consider it done! I have a few questions for you, but let me go see to this, and I will call you back for details."

As soon as Peter placed the phone in his pocket, he was hit with a new image. It was of a shoebox—a Nike shoebox, to be specific. In his mind's eye, he saw himself looking around the house and knew with absolute certainty that he needed to find that box!

Forty

Katie surprised herself with the enthusiasm in which she bounded up the stairs to her apartment. She knew she should feel tired but didn't. She was actually excited about the upcoming evening. For the first time in days, her thoughts were not revolving around her mom, Peter, or her family. She was completely focused on getting ready, what to wear . . . and yes . . . Shane.

After plugging Ally's phone into a charger, she grabbed an outfit from her closet and headed toward the bathroom. Getting dressed in the bathroom had become a habit while living in dorms, a habit she never broke. While the water in the shower was approaching a pleasant temperature, Katie carefully hung her outfit on the hook behind the bathroom door.

Edward, who had quietly made his way into the foyer area of the apartment, stood in the stairwell, straining to hear sounds from the apartment above. He heard a door close, followed by running water. He was certain she was taking a shower, which was perfect for him. *Pieces just keep falling into place.* Once again, it was as if fate took over for him. She would not be able to hear him moving about if she was in the shower. He couldn't see well into the unlit living room, so he used the dim light of his cell phone to guide him. He headed toward the sound of running water.

He fantasized about Katie but quickly reminded himself that this was a time for action, not anticipation or imagination. He was more than a little tempted to join her in the shower and have a little fun, but he resisted that urge. Patience . . . there would be plenty of time for pleasures later. For now, he had one mission to accomplish . . . one task . . . one job. The brief period of fantasizing caused beads of sweat to build up on his forehead. He took a deep breath and focused his mind on the one thing he had to do, which was quietly and discreetly get Katie back to his house. Alive!

As the shower stopped, he stood up against the wall. *The plan, focus on the plan! Stick to the plan!* The plan, the perfect plan—the plan in which Ethan is set up to take the fall for the deaths of Sharon, Katie, and all the others, the plan that would allow for Edward to scoot out of town, understandably broken and in need of a fresh start.

The letter was a key component of the plan, and thankfully when Ethan found the letter, he did exactly as Edward hoped he would, exactly what his mother had done when she found the box. He froze in a moment of panic, giving Edward the perfect opportunity to subdue him for the day. There was one major difference, though; Ethan dying was part of his plan, where Ethan's mom dying had not been part of the plan at all. He never intended for her to find the box. Actually, Edward had planned to grow old with her. But as life so often does, it had a plan of its own.

Edward was pleasantly surprised that fate's plan was as good as—or perhaps better than—his plan. Being a widower had its benefits. He was not just a widower, but he was the poor widower whose wife killed herself, leaving him with her weird son. This gained him a good deal of sympathy and allowed him to fly under the radar pretty easily, perhaps even more easily than being a simple family man. He was the guy frequently seen running errands around town, always cordial to the people he'd encounter, mostly keeping to himself, and this worked for him. It seemed like perfectly normal behavior for a man who'd been through all he had.

Unbeknownst to Ethan, his return presence in Edward's

life—his return visits to town—provided Edward with a do-over and an opportunity to wrap everything up, tie up all loose ends, and move on. However, Ethan would not be so lucky. Ethan would not be going anywhere.

It was one of the quickest showers Katie had ever taken, a far cry from the soothing, lingering one she had relished earlier in the day. Steam engulfed the bathroom mirror, making it necessary for Katie to dress not only quickly but blindly. She was dressed in a matter of minutes. Grateful that she learned to French braid her hair without the aid of a mirror, she took a few seconds to locate a hair tie that matched her outfit and secured it at the bottom of the braid. *This Shane just might be getting to me.* Satisfied with her hair, she turned and reached her hand toward the doorknob. The moment her hand came in contact with the metal knob, she was once again hit with a surge of fear and panic that coursed through her body so intensely that it left her paralyzed. Unable to move, she stood motionless, trying desperately to draw air into her lungs. *Breathe! Damn it, breathe!* After a minute, which felt more like an hour, Katie found herself able to catch her breath and move again. Oblivious to the fact that the door was only inches away from Edward, who was pressed to the wall waiting patiently for her, she twisted the knob and gingerly pushed the door open.

Forty-One

Peter entered the living room, where Patty was talking with Ethan. She was desperately trying to make sense of everything. "Sorry to interrupt, but I have a question for you, Ethan. I am looking for a box," Peter said.

Ethan gave a weak smile as he waved his arm toward a closed door. "That room is full of boxes. You want a box? Just open that door."

"Not just any box. I am looking for a particular box. I am looking for a black shoebox with a white Nike swish on it."

"Now that is one I have not seen. Why do you want that box? Need a pair of sneakers?" Ethan chuckled awkwardly.

"No," Peter responded weakly, He looked toward Patty and continued, "I wish I could tell you why I need it or what is in it, but I can't. I can only tell you I . . . or should I say we . . . need it. Of that I am certain. At least according to Sharon, or as you called her Mrs. Parish." As he spoke, the image of the shoebox filled his mind, and he heard Sharon's voice shouting, "*Find it! Find it!*"

"Mrs. Parish? Did he say Mrs. Parish?" Ethan's baffled voice filled the room.

"Yes, he did," Patty said calmly. Although she didn't fully understand what was going on, she no longer doubted Peter's hunches or Sharon's instructions. She gave Ethan an abridged version of what's been going on but was cut off by Peter.

"No time now." He held his hand up and continued, "Do you

mind if I have a look in that room?" As he was speaking, the image of the box flashed in his head.

"Sure, have at it. I'll come with you," Ethan said while standing up. He was a bit wobbly, but he was standing.

Patty reached for him, but he reassured her, looking steadier. "I'm okay . . . really, I'm good." He made his way across the room and opened the door for Peter. "In here. All my boxes are in here."

Peter entered the room as Ethan hit the light switch, and Peter found himself looking at the box that filled his head.

"What the hell?" Ethan stammered. "I've never seen that box before."

Peter cautiously approached the box, as if it may explode at any moment. He reached down and opened the lid. There was an immediate explosion—an explosion in his head. "Oh, my God," he said in a horrified, whispered tone. It was Peter who now looked unsteady as Ethan approached him. Wanting to protect Ethan and Patty from seeing the contents of the box, he instinctively and abruptly closed the lid. While trying to process the meaning of what he'd just seen, a new image formed in his mind. It was an image of him handing this box over to Officer O'Malley. The image was accompanied by Sharon's voice instructing him, "*Go! Go now!*" In the background, he could see the hourglass emptying.

"What's in there? Let me see!" Ethan said while reaching for the box.

"No!" Peter said forcefully, holding the box tightly to his body. "This box is coming with me."

"Where?" Ethan asked.

"To the police station," Peter answered while heading toward the door.

Patty could tell by the look on his face that there was no stopping him. She also knew she wanted—no, needed—to go with him, but she didn't want to leave Ethan alone. She looked at Ethan and said, "You need to trust us, okay? Come with us! Please!"

Forty-Two

Edward was eyeing the doorknob. *It's game time!* He closed his lips tightly to hold the air in his lungs. The door slowly swung back toward the wall and stopped in a half-open position, keeping him hidden. Readying himself, he retrieved the chloroform-soaked cloth from the container in his coat pocket. Silently, he inched his way closer to Katie. As soon as he was within striking distance, he raised the cloth to bring it around her mouth and nose.

BRRRRRNNGGGG.

The unexpected blaring of the alarm made Katie jump and turn around, bringing her face-to-face with Edward, who was also taken by surprise by the noise coming from the alarm clock. Edward lunged forward to get her to breathe in the chloroform. He grabbed Katie by the arm with his left hand while trying to bring the cloth in his right hand over her face. Katie resisted and yanked her arm free from his grasp. She stomped her foot down on his foot and pushed on his chest with surprising force, which caused him to stumble. His arms flailed, and he tried to regain his balance to no avail. He fell into the nightstand positioned next to Katie's bed before crashing into the wall. In the middle of the commotion, a female voice filled the apartment—"Run, Katie, run!" Without hesitation, Katie obeyed the faceless command and made her way out of the bedroom and down the stairs.

Half running, half falling, Katie made her way down the darkened staircase. As soon as her feet hit the bottom landing, she put her hand on the doorknob, and as she twisted it, she was met with resistance. A hand covered her mouth and pulled her close. She felt metal on her back, which she instinctively knew was a gun. Before she could struggle to get away, the man said in a whisper, "Shhhh . . . Officer Murphy here. You're safe. Is there someone up there?" Katie frantically nodded yes, and almost simultaneously, the officer pushed her out of the door and onto the porch, where she was greeted by two other uniformed individuals. One was a large male who handed her off to a female officer before joining Officer Murphy inside. With an arm on Katie's shoulder, the female officer, Officer Laney, guided Katie through the yard and to a patrol car.

"Are you okay? Are you injured?"

"No . . . no . . . I'm fine? Who is that? Wh . . . wha . . . what's going on?"

"I was hoping you could tell us. We . . ."

Screams of "Police! Don't move" coming from the porch cut the officer off mid-sentence. The yelling was followed by officers running onto the porch and into the house. Katie looked around and realized that police cars were surrounding the house, and groups of people gathered across the street.

While Katie was struggling to take in the scene, two police officers exited the building with a man in handcuffs. It was the man she had just escaped from. A shiver ran down her spine as she watched the man being escorted to a waiting police car. Another police officer yelled from the porch, "The house is clear!"

Katie looked confused and stammered out the question, "Ally? Where is Ally?"

"Was there someone else in the apartment?" the officer asked Katie.

"No . . . yes . . . um . . . I didn't think so, but she must be. She screamed for me to run. She must have come home."

The officer who handed her over to Officer Laney returned from the house and was walking toward them. He turned and yelled, "Hey, Herb. She says there is another female in the house."

"Nope! Not unless she is invisible. Entire house has been searched, and it's not that big. It was just that one guy. And he made it easy to catch him. He came flying down the stairs, ran right into Murph, almost knocked his scrawny ass over," he said with a chuckle.

"But . . . she yelled for me to run. She had to be there," Katie exclaimed.

"Ma'am, officers are finishing the canvas of the outside area, and while they are doing that, we will take another look inside. Just to put your mind at ease. While we do that, why don't you let Maria check you out?"

Katie was still trying to process everything that had just happened—the man in the apartment, the alarm going off, someone screaming for her to run, the police being here. She hadn't called them. *How did they know to come?* Maria and Katie were joined by Officer Murphy, who grabbed Katie and got her safely out of the apartment. He informed them it was all clear and proceeded to ask Katie if she was alright. Katie assured him she was fine but insisted that there was someone else in the house. Maria said in a soothing voice, "I'm sure you heard a voice yelling for you to run. It was probably your voice screaming in your head. Amazing what our bodies will do in response to stress."

"Katie! Katie!" Ally came sprinting across the yard toward her. The two girls met in an embrace.

While Katie and Ally stood five feet from the two officers, Officer Murphy said to Maria, "That is a good theory you shared with her. One problem, though. It doesn't explain how I heard the voice too."

"Oh, my God! What's going on? Are you alright? What the hell?" Ally said, talking fast, even for her.

"Some guy was in the apartment and tried to grab me."

"What? Who? Why?"

"Don't know!

Ally handed Katie her phone. "Here, this is why I ran over here. Your dad has been calling incessantly!" As soon as the phone hit the flesh on her hand, it vibrated. Katie answered the call.

"Dad?"

"Katie! Katie! Where are you? Are you okay?"

"I'm fine."

"Listen, I don't want to scare you, but we have reason to believe you might be in danger. Just don't be alone. I am on my way."

"Don't worry, Dad. I am definitely not alone. By the way, don't panic when you turn down my street."

Forty-Three

From the driver's seat of the car, Peter answered Ethan's questions as best he could, given his own struggles to understand what was happening. There was still so much that he didn't understand. *Was Edward a murderer? A serial killer? Was he responsible for Sharon's death? Katie's?* He pushed the last thought out of his mind as he struggled to explain the situation to Ethan. As the story unfolded, Ethan's doubts seemed to fade.

"I'm not sure what I think or believe, but there is no denying that you two showing up at the house . . . well . . . saved me . . . and hopefully Kat . . ."

Peter's cell phone rang loudly, cutting Ethan off. Peter said into his Bluetooth, "Hello." Ethan and Patty sat silently, trying to make sense of the one-sided conversation. The brief time in which Peter was on the phone felt like an eternity to Patty, who was sitting perfectly still, holding her breath, and waiting to hear news on Katie.

"She's okay! Katie's okay!" Peter said with the enthusiasm typically reserved to announce the birth of a baby.

"Oh, thank God! Where is she?" Patty exclaimed.

"She is at her apartment, but there are officers with her."

"And Edward?"

"He is in custody, and officers are bringing him to the station, according to O'Malley."

Patty immediately called John. She filled John in on the events of the evening, and he was relaying the information to Katie. She did not mention the box that was in the trunk, the box that Peter would not let anyone see the contents of. Patty could not imagine—or maybe was too frightened to imagine—what was in that box. All she knew was that Katie was safe and Edward was in custody. That knowledge enabled her to breathe a little easier.

Forty-Four

As John sat next to his only child, he was filled with so many questions. He was so grateful that she was safe and sound but still confused as to what was going on. They decided to go to the police station so Katie could give her statement and answer their questions. John talked with Patty and heard that they were also on their way to the police station and had Ethan with them. Until talking to Patty, he assumed that Ethan was the intruder in Katie's apartment. He turned to Katie and said, "Are you okay?" He couldn't stop asking her this question.

"I'm fine, really. A bit confused but fine. I wonder where Patty and Peter are."

"They are in a meeting with an officer. He's a friend of Peter's, the one who sent the police to your apartment just because Peter asked him to." John cringed at the thought of what might have happened had the police not been there. "They should be out short—" John was interrupted by an officer, who opened the door and approached Katie.

"Thanks for coming down. I'm Officer Johnson. Sorry to keep you waiting, but it's been one of those nights. If you follow me, we will get you out of here as quickly as possible." He looked toward John and told him he could wait right there. "The way things are going, it shouldn't be too long," Officer Johnson said.

"Okay," John replied, appearing more relaxed than he felt.

As Katie exited through one door, the familiar face of Patty entered the room through an adjacent door. She ran over to John and hugged him. "It's going to be okay. She's alright. She's alright."

"I know! Now for the million-dollar question. Why would Mr. Crow go after Katie?" John asked Patty.

"They are in there now trying to figure that out. I came out to see you and check on Ethan. He is in a room over there getting checked out by medical," Patty said, pointing down a long hallway to their left.

"Okay, you go check on Ethan. I'm going to wait here for Katie. For the record, I may sound like I have a clue, but in all honesty, I'm more confused than ever."

"Join the club," Patty said while heading down the hall.

◆ ◆ ◆

Peter stood in the office with O'Malley, nervously pacing the floor in front of the desk that O'Malley was sitting behind. He was on the phone with a detective who was going to be interrogating Edward.

"Has he lawyered up?" O'Malley asked into the phone. He was silent for a moment before replying, "Okay. Keep me posted."

O'Malley hung up the phone and directed his attention toward Peter, who was pacing in front of the desk. "Okay, now I have some questions for you."

Peter stopped pacing, placed his hand on the top of the desk, and leaned forward. "I bet you do!" As soon as the words left Peter's lips, he caught sight of a paper on the desk. The moment he saw the missing girl flier, he could once again hear Sharon's voice screaming, *"Help her! Save her!"*

We did, Sharon. We saved her. He was immediately gripped with panic and fear. Once again, Sharon's voice filled his head. *"Save her! Find her! Please!"*

He reached his hand down and grabbed the flier. As soon as he touched it, his usual abilities took over. He saw Beth lying in a heavily wooded area by the lake. She was injured and cold, but she was alive. Peter was sure of that. He was also sure he could locate her. O'Malley, seeing the look on Peter's face as he held the flier, stared at him when Peter finally said, "She is alive! This Beth girl is alive!"

"What?"

"Listen, we don't have time to waste. She is alive, and I believe I can help you find her, but we have to go find her! Now!"

"Alright. I'll get a car to pick us up out back."

"Us?"

"You betchya. I'm coming with you. My shift here is almost done. Not just my shift. My career is almost done. Let's just say I have a vested interest in this one!"

"Alright, but I don't think she is close by. I don't believe that she is in your jurisdiction!"

"Of course not!" O'Malley sighed. "I will get someone to wrap things up here and meet you in the back parking lot. We can take my car!"

Peter hurried toward the exit and stopped when he spotted Patty. She was in the hallway talking to a medic, who had just told her they wanted Ethan to go to the hospital to be checked out further. He was assuring her it was precautionary, and he was most likely fine. Peter quickly told Patty about Beth and his certainty that she was still alive. He instructed Patty to take his car to the hospital with Ethan.

"Keep me posted . . . please!" Patty implored.

"I will. You do the same," Peter replied while heading to the exit.

Forty-Five

O'Malley did not have the luxury of enjoying his last departure from the police station as he rushed out the door and down the steps to the parking lot. He had done this type of thing with Peter before, but it was always in the line of duty, not like this, as a private citizen, driving his own car into another town. For all he knew, he could be going to another state. *Carol is going to kill me for not coming straight home.* He pulled the car around to pick up Peter, who was on the sidewalk waiting for him.

"We need to get on the highway and head toward Miller Road," Peter said with confidence.

"Got it," O'Malley replied while pulling the car onto the road. Having assisted Peter on prior occasions, he knew to refrain from making small talk or asking unnecessary questions. He remained silent as he pulled onto the highway. As it often does, the crisp, sunny autumn day had transformed into a cold and rainy night. The rain, although not falling terribly hard, added to the difficulty of the task at hand. O'Malley considered calling Carl, but everything was happening so fast. He didn't have the time, and he wasn't sure what he'd tell him since he wasn't sure what was going on.

Twenty minutes into the drive, Peter felt a sudden wave of nausea. *Not now! Please, not now!* He was pleading with his body not to succumb to the nausea. He rolled the window down, allowing for cold pellets of rain to hit his face. On this stretch of the lake, there were no beautiful lakeside cottages or wineries. The land surrounding this section of the lake was unforgiving and not conducive to building on.

The landscape ranged from steep hills to complete cliffs that abruptly dropped into the lake. There was no beach area here; the heavily wooded land just fell into the water, which ranged from thirty to fifty feet in depth. Although the lake was not far beyond the road, it was not easily accessible.

Looking out the open passenger window, the familiarity of the location hit Peter like a sledgehammer. It was the exact spot in which he felt ill while driving to and from his reading event at Mrs. K's. With the rain pellets stinging his face and Sharon screaming for him to "*Help her,*" Peter held Beth's picture tight and focused intently. The images came rushing in fast and clear. He knew they were close. The silence in the car ended abruptly as Peter began to give Patrick directions.

"Take a right here . . . turn down the dirt road . . . head toward the lake . . . and stop!" Peter hopped out of the car as soon as it came to a stop.

"Wait up!" O'Malley hollered, pulling a flashlight out and shining it in Peter's direction.

"She's here!" Peter said to O'Malley before yelling out her name. "Beth! Beth! Are you here?"

The two men called out in unison while heading slowly and carefully through the cold and wet woods. "Beth! Beth! Can you hear us?"

The rain stopped, but water was still dripping from the trees. The temperature, which was warm earlier in the day, dropped a good thirty degrees, and the water stung as it encountered bare skin.

"Come on, this way," Peter said, pointing toward a small slope leading to the lake.

"Be careful!" O'Malley replied.

"She's here . . . I know she's here." Just as the men were ready to call out again, they heard a voice.

"Here . . . I'm here . . . help me . . . please!"

That was all they needed to locate Beth. As Peter slid down the small but slippery slope, he saw the body of a young girl lying near a tree next to the lake. "Beth?"

"Yes," Beth said through tears. "Oh, thank God, you found me!"

"Are you hurt?" Peter asked.

"My leg. My leg is hurt bad. I can't get up."

"Okay, we got you now," Peter said while finally reaching her. She was cold and shaken and had a badly broken leg, but she was alive! "It's okay. We are going to get you out of here. My name is Peter, and the man coming down the hill now is Officer O'Malley."

"Here is a jacket and a blanket," O'Malley said while handing the items to Peter. "I also brought a bottle of water. The ambulance is on the way, along with the police."

Peter covered Beth up with the coat and blanket, and then he helped her with the bottle of water. It wasn't long before they could hear sirens in the distance.

"If you guys are good here, I'm going to meet them so I can lead them here," O'Malley said.

"We are good."

Beth looked up at Peter and said, "I don't know who you are or how you found me, but thank you." Tears fell down her face. "I don't know what happened, but that man . . . that man . . . in the car . . . last thing I remember . . . until . . . until . . . I was in the water with something pulling me down. Something on my leg . . . pulling me down . . . couldn't breathe . . . cold . . . going to die. She helped me! She made me swim! She pushed me up . . . out of the water."

"Who did? Beth, who helped you?" Peter asked.

"Not sure, but I think it was my guardian angel."

Peter couldn't argue with that logic as he thought of Sharon.

"It's okay, Beth. You're safe now, and you are not going to die. Just relax and take it easy."

The sirens sounded as if they were right next to them, and before Peter knew it, a crew was there, stabilizing her leg. A few minutes later, she was lifted onto a gurney. Peter helped the men navigate the wooded area as they slowly made their way toward the ambulance. Before the ambulance pulled away, one attendant informed Peter and O'Malley that they would be taking Beth to General Hospital in Granderson Falls.

"I have to call my friend who knows Beth and her family," O'Malley said.

"Okay. I have a call to make myself."

Peter took one last look at the lake. The lights of the homes and cottages across the lake were very visible. Peter reached into his pocket and pulled out his phone, but before placing a call to Patty, he opened Google Maps. His hunch was confirmed. Directly across the water on the east side of the lake sat The Crow's Nest.

Six Months Later

Forty-Six

Her legs were burning, but in a good way. She felt strong and determined. It was a picture-perfect day for running—sixty-two degrees, with just enough cloud cover to allow the sun to brighten the day without making it unbearably hot. Katie had long since left Ally behind. Her plan was to run the entire 26.2 miles alongside Ally, but Ally had another plan in mind. She wanted very much for Katie to qualify to run in the Boston Marathon, and she knew she could do it! She made her point crystal clear as they were warming up in preparation for the day's run.

That conversation was playing in Katie's mind as she began the last three miles of the race. She felt fantastic.

That was not the case a few miles back when she wasn't even sure she would finish the race, never mind post a time that would qualify her to run in Boston. At that point, her legs were on fire, and she could not find the oxygen she so desperately needed, which led to her breathing being way off. She mumbled toward the sky, "C'mon girl, you dedicated this race to your mom. What did she yell at you that night? Run, Katie, run!" Katie rolled those three words over in her mind as she managed to put one foot in front of the other and breathe in and out. Left foot . . . air in . . . right foot . . . air out . . . left foot . . . run, Katie, run . . . left foot . . . Before she knew it, her legs were no longer struggling to move. She had found her second wind, more like a sixth wind, but she found it, and she was moving. "This one's for you, Mom!" she said to the sky.

As she turned the corner and headed into the final stretch, she felt as though she was running on air. Although she could not see them yet, she knew, somewhere in the crowd around the finish line, her own cheering section waited. It was a new, albeit welcomed, change for her to be running toward something rather than running away. She was running toward her future, toward her family, toward her friends, which included Ethan, and Shane, who had become more than just a friend. The thought of Shane made her legs move faster, and she passed the one runner she saw in front of her. As she was overtaking the now struggling runner, she heard an eruption of cheers, which only made her run faster. Arms raised over her head, she crossed the line and was met with applause and shouts of congratulations.

"You are the first female to finish!" Shane said while giving her a hug.

"Holy shit, you not only qualified . . . you won!" Ally chimed in. "We are going to Boston!"

As Katie hydrated and caught her breath, she was congratulated by fellow runners and spectators. Her dad, Patty, and Peter stood back and took in the moment.

What a great way to spend the day, six months after "the night," as they referred to it, the night that Katie and her family found answers that solved the mystery of what happened to Sharon twelve years ago. Along with the Parish family, so many other families had their mysteries solved. So many questions were answered. Closure was brought to so many people, including Ethan.

It was still hard to imagine Edward as a serial killer. The thought still sent chills up her spine. Once Edward was taken into custody from Katie's apartment, it was as if a dam had broken. Edward made the detective's work not just easy but unnecessary. He didn't want a lawyer—he just wanted to talk. It almost appeared as if he wanted to brag. He was more than willing to give up all the gory details.

When shown the box of pictures Peter found, Edward methodically went through each one and told the story of how each of his victims left this world, which led to many families receiving the horrible news that their missing loved ones were, in fact, dead. It also led to the recovery of many bodies. Beth was the one bright spot of the entire ordeal. Her picture was not in the box, but only because it was in Edward's possession. When he was shown the picture of Beth taken from his belongings, he described how he encountered her while returning from picking up Ethan's car from the shop. He talked about having to rush because of Ethan being around. He sent Ethan out to get dinner so he could take the boat across the lake, where he could dump the unconscious girl with a cinder block tied to her leg into the lake. The detective questioning Edward was ecstatic to hear that she had miraculously been found and was safe.

It turned out that Sharon was his biggest disappointment, which is why he was so excited and convinced that Katie was his second chance. A do-over was how he referred to it.

Sharon was dead before he even got off her street. He figured she had an adverse reaction to the chloroform and died immediately. He recounted the night with extraordinarily little emotion. He knocked on the door. When Sharon opened it, he looked upset and said he was sorry to bother her, but he was very worried about Ethan. Opening a sketch pad, he said to her, "Look what he drew." As she stepped out and leaned closer to look, he placed the chloroform cloth over her face. Her body went limp. He quietly closed the door and escorted her to the BMW he drove on occasions like this. While driving the winding lakeside road home, he became aware that something was wrong. A quick check told him he was right; she was gone.

Edward brought Sharon to the rowboat, placed her lifeless

body in the boat, and quietly rowed from the shore to where the lake was two hundred feet deep. He secured two cinder blocks to her and rolled her body into her lake grave. With sadness for his failed plan, he sipped a beer as he slowly and quietly made his way home.

John, Patty, and Katie found some peace knowing that Sharon felt no pain and left this world peacefully—much too soon but peacefully. They held a memorial service on a boat they rented. It was a small group that included Ethan, Ally, and Peter. They took turns saying their goodbyes. Peter shared that while they were speaking to Sharon, he saw the broken heart he had been seeing, but it was being mended together and seemed to glow. The broken heart faded away, and an image of Sharon standing with a man appeared. Peter instantly recognized the familiar figure. It was his dad. He was smiling and appeared happy as he looked lovingly at Peter. Sharon's voice filled Peter's head; *"He loves you and is very proud of you."* Peter was enveloped with a warm feeling as the image faded. He decided to keep this treasured message to himself.

Mary, Ethan's mom, was the one anomaly. Edward had every intention of staying married and growing old with her, but when she discovered his box of pictures, he had to act quickly, and act quickly he did. Knowing she would panic and take off, he grabbed a cloth and soaked it in chloroform. He snuck up behind her and placed it over her mouth. While she was out cold, he grabbed his bottle of Ambien and ground them into a drink. As she came to, he managed to get the water and vodka, along with six or so additional pills, down her throat before hitting her with another brief smell of chloroform. As she passed out, he used gloves to place the bottle in one hand and the vodka glass in the other, remaining pills spread around her. He took off to work, leaving her for Ethan to find. Ethan, who had always thought it was just an unfortunate act of desperation on his mom's part, something he carried guilt for, was given the news that she was murdered by the man she married.

Katie was not thinking of Edward as she was greeted by family and friends at the finish line. She knew what he did would never make sense, no matter how often she thought about it, so she tried not to give Edward or his atrocious acts much thought. Instead, she was grateful for the closure and choose to focus on the good in her life along with the many beautiful memories.

◆ ◆ ◆

The congratulations continued to flow over dinner, but this time they were not directed at Katie. They were being given to Peter and Patty, who had just shocked the table when Peter raised his glass and toasted to him and Patty on their engagement. Patty interrupted the chorus of congratulations. "Hold on a second. There's more."

"You're not going to tell us you're pregnant, are you?" John's words elicited laughter from the table.

"Nope." Patty chuckled. "Peter and I have decided to sell our homes and are embarking on an adventure of our own. We are going to travel this beautiful country in our RV," she said, unable to contain her excitement.

"You have an RV?" Katie asked.

"Why yes, we do!" Patty said, unable to contain her smile.

"And she is a beaut!" Peter chimed in. "In fact, we are staying here in her tonight if you would like to see her."

"Here? You are camping here?" John asked.

"Yes, we are. They have spots for RVs overlooking the vineyards. We thought since we were coming here for the race, it would be a great time to break her in! Which brings us to the next surprise."

"You mean there's more?" John asked.

Patty, who looked like the cat who swallowed the canary, replied, "Yes, there is, and if someone would ask when our wedding date is . . ."

"When is the date?" Katie asked excitedly.

"Well, we'd rather show you than tell you, so when everyone is done eating, that is exactly what we will do."

"Really? You are going to tease us and keep us in suspense?" Katie pouted.

"Absolutely!" Peter and Patty said in unison.

The table grew quiet as everyone began stuffing food into their mouths.

An hour later, with the sun setting over the lake, Peter and Patty stood at the edge of the vineyard. Surrounded by family and a few close friends, they became Mr. and Mrs. Dorjen. The event that Peter and Patty planned weeks before went exactly as they envisioned. When the ceremony concluded, Peter led the small group on a tour of their new home on wheels, a beautiful Prevost. The inside was amazingly homey. It had a nice kitchen, theater seating, a large TV on a Televator, and a gorgeous electric fireplace. It was the type of motorhome that celebrities used to travel the country.

"She's a beauty, isn't she?"

"Oh, my God, it is gorgeous!" Katie beamed. "When do you two plan on hitting the road?"

"We finish all our business here in a couple of weeks, and then we are heading out," Peter replied.

"Where's the first destination?"

"South Dakota!" Patty said enthusiastically. "I have always wanted to see Mount Rushmore."

"And I have always wanted to see Devils Tower!" Peter chimed in.

Inside the newly married couple's RV, the group raised their glasses to the new couple, to adventures, and, of course, to Sharon.

ACKNOWLEDGMENTS

I must begin with my wonderful, patient, and supportive husband, Bart, who was as important to this book getting done as I was. From his willingness to read and provide honest feedback to being my one-man tech support, this book never would have come to fruition without him, and if by some miracle it did, I am sure it would have been accidentally deleted or lost in the cloud somewhere. Love you, honey!

I must mention my late dear friend, Susan Carberry, who left us much too soon. Her excitement, support, and insight were highly motivating, allowing for me to push through the tough times, not only in writing but in life. I am so grateful for her help and support and beyond thankful that she was around to celebrate my signing with Koehler Books. Although I am deeply saddened that she is not here to share in the publication process with me, I take pride and find peace in knowing that I have a fan with wings cheering me on from above!

Louise Levasseur, I thank you for going above and beyond time and time again—reading, editing, consulting, and putting your years of business experience to use, guiding me through the publishing process!

My wonderful group of readers—beginning with my initial small group of readers and supporters, Amy Balash, Sandy Ercolani, Therese Hourihan and Nancy Miles. Next, my beta readers— Nancy Bahr, Bonnie Dibble, Laurie Hobler, Nichole Inthanongsak, Linda Maloney, Carol McDaniel, Linda Stundtner, and Karen Whitman. Your feedback, insight, and encouragement were invaluable! Book two is heading your way!

John and Tami Rossignol, thank you for making the dreaded headshot experience fun and managing to make this unphotogenic girl look like a rock star! Also, I am grateful for your help in promoting the book!

Thank you, Nicholas Harvey, for taking the time to share your knowledge and experiences with me.

To the entire team at Koehler Books, John Koehler and Greg Fields for seeing the potential in my writing and taking a chance on a fifty-nine-year-old rookie, Miranda Dillon whose editing skills helped *Run! Katie!* reach that full potential, Christine Kettner who worked on the cover design as well as formatting, and Anna Torres for getting the book out in the world! Thank you all for playing a role in my dream coming true!

A heartfelt thanks to everyone who reads this book. I only hope you enjoy reading it half as much as I enjoyed writing it!

My last thank you comes in the form of a shout-out to the heavens, "Thank you Mom and Dad for everything! You are missed and thought of daily!"